Dandelion Seeds

A Collection of Short Stories
by Steve DeGroof
Edited by Amanda Sternbergh

Contents

Foreword

In January 2016, there was a hashtag going around Twitter: #FirstLineToMyNovel. Being a smartass, I wrote 18 of them. A few weeks later, I created a tumblr with a post for each of those lines, and added a plausible title, without knowing where the story might go.

Over the next couple months, I tried to flesh out each one into a short story, using my usual "first draft is good enough" writing technique.

One of those lines was similar enough to a story I'd already written, so I just went ahead and posted it.

With the rest, I began adding to them a bit at a time, as time and inspiration allowed.

Just to make things interesting, I set up some rules for me to follow:

1. Use the line from the tweet, verbatim, as the first line of the story.

2. Write start-to-finish. No rewrites or major edits. Clean up grammar and spelling only.

3. Write the stories on Tumblr itself. No writing offline.

For the record, I broke each of those rules at least once, but tried to stick to them anyway.

Dandelion Seeds

Karen once again found herself wondering how she'd ended up captain of a ship crewed by 500 nerds and one insane A.I. She unstrapped herself from her bunk and drifted over to the console.

"Genie: The usual," she commanded. A few seconds later, the console dispensed a flask of black coffee and something that could arguably be called a blueberry muffin.

This was a big step up from the state of Genie's voice interface when they'd first started using it. The A.I. was, at best, experimental. At worst, it was dangerously unpredictable. The phrase, "the usual" was a shortcut she'd trained it to understand in order to avoid having to specify every single detail of the order. 500ml of water heated to 98C, mixed with 20ml beverage concentrate #237, and so on.

With Genie, much like its legendary namesakes, you had to be careful what you asked for. The crew learned this the hard way early on, when Kazniki glibly commanded, "Genie: make me a sandwich." They held a funeral and burial-at-space for him …after extracting his remains from between two large slices of bread.

Karen finished her blueberry muffin-ish thing, washed it down with the remaining coffee, drifted over to the door to her room, braced herself, slid it open and…

"Captain Durning! Ma'am!" Cartwright snapped a salute, beaming. Just like she did every morning. Or afternoon. Or, really, every *fucking* time Karen happened to run into Cartwright. Which was a *lot*. The kid was underfoot all the time. Well, as much as you *could* be underfoot in microgravity.

"Morning, Cartwright," Karen said. "What's the latest?"

"The Athena is going to try out their jump drive today!" Cartwright said excitedly. "This will change *everything*!"

Oh god. The Athena, Minerva's sister ship, was similarly crewed by a bunch of nerds, and for the same reason. Pete Hanson, their de facto captain, was quite a bit more ambitious …and reckless. Decent guy and all, but a bit too eager to latch onto the "next big thing". When one of his crew suggested that Genie (their instantiation of the Genie A.I.) be used to design a faster-than-light propulsion system, Hanson jumped on it. They'd spent the past month carefully outlining the parameters under which the jump drive should work and feeding them into the A.I. Given Genie's uncanny tendency to provide unexpected results, this seemed like a BAD IDEA.

"They're going to get themselves killed," Karen half-mumbled.

"Oh, no. They'll be fine." said Cartwright. "At least I *hope* so. I have a good feeling about this. They're about to try a short jump. Shall we go watch, ma'am?"

Cartwright launched herself toward the window nearest Athena. Karen followed, a bit less gracefully. The kid really seemed at home in microgravity. Kid? The records said Cartwright was 23 years old, but she *looked* like a kid. Well, a six foot tall, gangly tech-genius kid. Cartwright had a very child-like face, wide-eyed with delicate features. Very pretty, in a weirdly exotic way. And she meticulously maintained a purple dye job, including eyebrows and lashes. Karen couldn't remember ever seeing any roots showing. And those eyes – so light brown they were almost golden. Had to be tinted lenses.

Karen was pulled out of her musings by an audio transmission from Athena. She pressed her face to the window to get a good look at the ship, barely more than a speck at this distance.

"Ten, nine, eight…"

This is going to go horribly wrong.

"Five, four, three, two, one."

The speck was suddenly slightly to the right of where it had been. Cheering could be heard over the audio link, and from her own crew.

"Holy fuck," she whispered. "They did it."

She glanced over at Cartwright who, oddly, appeared to be fiddling with her phone rather than joining in the festivities. She shrugged. Probably texting a boyfriend or something. There were certainly plenty of eligible young men on board.

In fact, nearly everyone on board was gorgeous, or at least extremely photogenic. Both men and women. The same was true of the Athena. It was as if someone had hand-picked the most attractive nerds on the planet to work on the space ships. And that was almost certainly what had happened.

See, the Athena and Minerva were supposed to be lifeboats. Earth was doomed, they said. Comet collision imminent, they said. We need to build life boats to save the best of humanity from almost certain doom. Of course, the rich and powerful naturally assumed that the best of humanity was… well… the rich and powerful. So they made sure *they* had tickets for the voyage.

The problem was that most of those particular "best of humanity" folks couldn't figure out how to swing a hammer without being shown which end to aim at the nail. And the Athena and Minerva were considerably more complicated than the average hammer. So, they needed nerds. They chose a thousand – five hundred for each ship – to get the systems in order before launch. The ships had been built in orbit but still needed to be wired up – communications, food prep, sanitation bots, all the little techie things that make life comfortable. Nearly everyone chosen jumped at the chance because, a) it was a chance to work in space and b) you had about a 25% chance of actually going on the voyage.

The rich bastards who'd chosen themselves as the, erm, chosen ones, had estimated they'd need about 120 techs to stay on board to maintain the systems. The lucky few would be chosen by lottery.

So why did the pool of candidates consist almost exclusively of very attractive people? No one ever came out and said it, but Karen's guess was that they would be expected to double as "eye candy" for the ships' primary occupants. Knowing that, she signed up anyway. It was creepy as fuck but still better than being hit in the face by a comet … probably.

But then two very unexpected events happened. Actually, one unexpected event happened and one expected one didn't.

First, the ships launched six months early. Accidentally. Despite several fail-safe systems being in place, both ships launched accidentally, simultaneously, six months early. Just after the last of the supplies were loaded, but *before* the first residents boarded. Very precise and *criminally suspicious* timing, Karen thought. And by the time anyone could figure out how to stop the launch, it was too late to turn around and go back. There were frantic messages from Earth but, really, what could they do? What could anyone do? So the ships launched with only five hundred on each, far less than the thousands it was equipped to accommodate. A total of a thousand nerds were the last hope for humanity. *God help us.*

The other thing that happened – or, more to the point, failed to happen – was the comet. No comet. No impact. Nothing. Well, not *nothing*. Shortly after the date the comet would have hit, there were reports of a global pandemic. By this time Minerva and Athena had been on their way for half a year. Signals were weak and, frankly, no one was really motivated to keep the ships up to date on world events. It wasn't long before the signals stopped altogether.

The assumption by those on board was that a disease had wiped out the rest of the human race. A disease that *just happened* to break out about the time of the supposed comet event. Almost as if, say, a bunch of rich powerful assholes had conspired to build space ships, hop on board, kill off the riff-raff, then come back in twenty years or so when the air was safe to breathe again.

So, then, why didn't they stop the outbreak when they realized they didn't have an escape plan? Was it too late? Were events already in motion? What sort of disease could be set up as a time bomb *and couldn't* be defused? That bit bugged Karen more than anything. She could believe the genocidal conspiracy, but who the fuck doesn't build in a back-out plan?

All of that was two years ago. Two years since the last indication of live humans on Earth had reached the ships.

Karen realized she'd been staring off into space – literally – for several minutes now. No one seemed to have noticed. They were all too busy celebrating Athena's successful jump. Right. The jump. She glided back to her ready room, shut the door, and opened a private video link to Captain Hanson.

"Well, Pete, you managed not to blow yourself up again," she grinned at him.

"Hey, it worked. I told you it would. I believe you owe me a dollar," he said.

"You'll have to come over here to get it."

"I just might do that, now that my ship *can go anywhere she likes*." He was really rubbing it in. "But first, I want to take her out for a spin, see what she can do."

"Go slowly, please," she cautioned.

"Yeah, yeah. Just a quick hop to the nearest star and back," he said, trying to sound as casually disinterested as possible.

"You're going to get yourself killed, you know that?"

"Naw, we'll be fine. But, hey, I'm sending a data packet over. The specs for the jump drive. Figured you should have a copy, just in case." So, he was at least a little worried. Still stupidly incautious, though.

"Thanks. But, look, do me a favor. Whatever you're going to do, wherever you're going, just go there and immediately come back. No poking around. Not for this trip anyway. Just there and back. And signal us as soon as you return. Safety first, OK?"

Pete sighed. "Yeah, sure. Makes sense. That way, you can verify it works. Also, you can time us and see how goddamn fast this thing is," he grinned.

She laughed. "OK. Just… have a safe trip."

"Aye aye Captain!" He mock-saluted her and signed off.

Dandelion Seeds

Karen exited her ready room again. The bridge had filled up quite a bit, presumably as news of the successful test had spread. And the bridge definitely had the best view of Athena. The forward half of the sphere that made up the bridge was made up almost entirely of windows.

Also, most of the living space on the ship was in the Donut, the huge, rotating torus aft of the bridge. The rotation made for nice, comfortable living but also made it nearly impossible to keep your eyes on anything outside the ship.

Karen rarely left the bridge, preferring microgravity to the half-gee artificial gravity of the Donut. The rotation played hell on her inner ears, making her stumble at best and, at worst, puke her guts out. She visited there only enough to exercise her muscles and keep them from atrophying. Also, the bridge was usually pretty quiet.

Right now, though, it was packed. Crowded enough that people were drifting into each other. And with bodies oriented every which way, some of the collisions were awkward and embarrassing. She heard quite a few of yelps and mortified apologies among the chatter.

She also heard a steady countdown from Athena's audio link. As the count reached ten, Hanson's voice cut in with, "Watch this space. We'll be right back."

Three, two, one. The ship winked out of existence.

Everyone cheered.

Everyone waited.

And waited.

The bridge was nearly silent. If Pete was trying to make things dramatic, he was overdoing it.

OK, something was definitely wrong. She scanned the crowd and easily picked out her purple-haired wunderkind. "Cartwright! In my ready room, please."

The girl launched herself from her position across the bridge and easily navigated the maze of drifting bodies, half-flying, half-dancing her way through. Kid must've studied ballet at some point.

"Captain!" Cartwright drifted to a stop beside Karen, saluted, and waited to be invited in.

Once they were both inside, Karen looked Cartwright in the eyes and said, "OK, look, something's gone horribly wrong and we need to find out what and find out quickly. So, let's drop the formalities. Hell, I'm only captain because no one else wanted the job."

Cartwright opened her mouth to object but Karen shushed her.

"It's not important right now. From this point forward, I'm Karen, you're Ana. No salutes, no 'permission to speak freely ma'am', none of that. We're equals and we're working on a problem. Protocol will just get in the way. Got it?"

Ana nodded, wide-eyed. Even wider eyed than usual, which was saying something.

Karen pulled up the specs for the jump drive. "Athena sent me this just before they left. We've got to pick though it and find out what's broken. Because something is *definitely* broken."

"Yes ma..." Ana started, then saw Karen's look. "Yes."

They started picking through the maze of diagrams, equations and graphs. It looked like... Frankly, it looked like Albert Einstein, Vera Rubin and Grace Hopper had dropped acid and then tried to build a device for summoning demons.

"Holy shit..." said Karen, shaking her head.

"It's... very complicated," noted Ana. "It *was* designed by Genie, though, so I suppose it shouldn't be that surprising that it's a bit... eccentric."

"It's totally bat-shit. This here – that's an avocado, isn't it?" Karen pointed to a green object at the center of the navigation sub-unit. "What's an avocado... Do we even *have* avocados on board?"

"Oh yes! The arborium produces a few now and then. They're *wonderful*."

"Not really the point," Karen said, leaning back and rubbing her eyes. "We're never going to figure this out. How did the Athena manage this?"

Ana shrugged. "I think they just followed the build instructions."

"So, no one knows how it works. Fucking brilliant."

"There might be another approach we could take," suggested Ana. "Do we have the original requirements document fed into Genie?"

Karen stared at the girl. Smart kid. She really stood out from her peers, and not just because of the purple hair and general gangliness. "Right. They're in here somewhere…" She called up the index screen.

Wait… She really stood out. Something about that nagged at Karen. She shook her head. That'd have to wait.

The requirements doc started off fairly simple: get from *here* to *there* in the minimum amount of time. Taking into account Genie's tendency to come up with non-intuitive solutions, though, they'd added some very specific requirements on a lot of obvious things. No change in mass, size or topology, for example. No point in having an FTL drive that turns you inside out.

It looked like the materials requirements went through a few revisions. First "must use available materials", then "available expendable materials", then "available expendable *non-human* materials". Karen shuddered at that last bit.

"This is interesting," said Ana, pointing to the basic requirements section. "They've specified maximum elapsed time for two different frames of reference: ship time and time as experienced by an outside observer. Maximum one second on each."

"Seems reasonable," Karen said. "No point in the voyage taking an instant in ship's time if two hundred years had passed outside the ship."

Ana sighed the sigh of a nerd who's seen something *they* think is obvious and is now burdened with explaining it. "Sure. But on *every other* parameter – temperature, pressure, EM radiation all along the spectrum – they specified upper *and* lower bounds. On elapsed time, they missed, or skipped, the lower limit."

"So? The minimum is going to be…" began Karen. "Oh shit."

She turned to her console. "Genie," she commanded, "analyze the design in file archive JumpDrive3A."

DONE displayed the console screen. Genie could speak and even interact using an animated avatar but some jackass had reprogrammed the interface to look like a blonde in a harem outfit who referred to everyone as "master". So Karen stuck to text feedback. *I really need to find out who did that and figure out a suitable punishment.*

"OK, what would be the elapsed time of the Athena for a jump? List both subjective and objective times."

SUBJECTIVE: 0.37s ±0.005s
EXTERNAL: -58d/c ±2%

"OK, so, less than half a second, ship's time. Genie: Explain the result for the 'External' figure."

THE EXTERNAL ELAPSED TIME IS DEPENDENT ON THE DISTANCE TRAVELED. IT IS APPROXIMATELY THE DISTANCE TRAVELED, DIVIDED BY THE SPEED OF LIGHT, MULTIPLIED BY A FACTOR OF NEGATIVE FIFTY-EIGHT.

Karen could swear she heard a nerd-sigh from the console's speakers. "So, from our perspective, they traveled back in time? I didn't notice anything on their first jump. OK, let's do the math… The first one was, what, a hundred kilometers?"

Ana jumped in. "Right, so 100,000 meters, divided by 300,000,000 meters per second, times 58… About twenty milliseconds. No. *Negative* twenty milliseconds."

"You did that in your head? Jeez. Alright. That explains why we didn't notice. Any way to verify the result?" Karen asked, still hoping this was an error in Genie's calculations …and also avoiding thinking about the implications of the next result.

"Sure. They were traveling roughly parallel to Minerva at the time, and they had an open comm channel. Let me pull up the logs…" Ana tapped on the keyboard. The girl was probably the only human on board who trusted Genie *less* than Karen did.

"Yeah. Here. We had a sync error for, yes, about twenty milliseconds. And it looks like it was due to carrier interference. Transmission from Athena overlapped itself." Ana shrugged, palms-up: the universal "oh well" gesture.

This kid is really amazing, A real stand-out… Oh. Oh fuck.

"Ana," Karen began, turning the girl to face her, "Who are you, where did you come from, and how did you get on board?"

The girl looked shocked. "I… What?" she stammered.

"Something has been bugging me for ages and I couldn't quite put my finger on it," Karen said, letting go of Ana and drifting back a bit. "You. You stand out. Just before we came in here, I picked you out of a crowd instantly. On a ship filled entirely with people who, frankly, all look like catalog models, you're the only person who *doesn't*."

Karen anchored herself to her bunk. It's difficult to be dramatic when you're slowly tumbling in midair. She rubbed her eyes and tried to collect her thoughts. "I think… I think the only reason I hadn't noticed sooner is that you've pretty much been shadowing me the whole time. You've pretty much been underfoot since I was elected captain. Right after the accident. But the fact is, you don't fit the profile. You don't fit in."

She raised her head and looked Ana in the eyes – those weird golden eyes – looking for any sign of what the hell the girl was thinking. "And I just noticed you managed to get me monologuing without actually answering my questions. So, out with it. What's your deal?"

Ana's posture changed. Subtly, but there was a distinct difference in the way she held herself. She no longer looked shocked, or offended. She didn't even, as Karen had hoped, look guilty. She seemed, what, annoyed?

"Fine," Ana said, pulling out her phone absently. "My name really is Ana Cartwright. I'm from a place called Cartref, not that it helps. I came on board during the last cargo shipment. And, yes, I added myself to the ship's roster when I boarded."

Huh. "You're a stowaway. And you just *happened* to come on board right before the Accident. Did you cause the Accident? And while we're at it, I'm Captain of this ship and you're a stowaway, so I think the *least* you could do is pay attention to me and stop playing with your phone!"

Ana – the *stowaway* – calmly looked up from her phone. "OK," she said, tapped at it a few more times and pocketed it. "This isn't exactly the way we expected things to play out but it'll have to do. Let's go back out to the bridge. There's something I think you need to see."

"Sure, why not?!" Karen threw up her hands in exasperation, causing her to tumble again. "It's not like I'm *in charge* or anything!"

Ana slid the door open and launched herself into the bridge. Karen followed. The crowd had thinned out quite a bit, so the view was much better.

The bridge was roughly spherical, with the forward-facing hemisphere consisting almost entirely of interlocking windows. This was another reason Karen spent so much time in the ready room. She could pop out of her room at any time and look at the stars. *Best view on the ship.*

That view was suddenly, alarmingly blocked by a huge, silver, disc-shaped object. It was difficult to judge scale without knowing distance but it was clearly much bigger than Minerva.

"Oh *come on*!" Karen shouted over the gasps and panicked chattering of the bridge's remaining occupants. "A flying saucer?! *Really*?!" This was shaping up to be one of the weirdest days ever, and it wasn't even lunchtime yet.

And then, as if on cue, the day got weirder. A message in huge, white, translucent letters appeared in the space between the two ships. It read:

Greetings, Captain Durning.

The shock of being addressed directly by a giant flying saucer was almost overwhelming, but a small part of Karen's mind noted that the text was conveniently oriented so that it was upright relative to *her*. Also, they used correct punctuation, which made the message a bit more ordinary, almost comforting in a way. It wasn't even in some weird all-caps sci-fi typeface. It just looked like plain text. *Other than the fact that it's some sort of holographic projection from an alien ship,* a slightly more savvy part of her mind interjected.

"Is that Helvetica?" she said, half to herself.

Dandelion Seeds

Ana, right beside her (of course), replied, "Univers Bold, actually. It seemed appropriate."

Was that a smirk? Karen gestured at the scene in front of them. "You seem to know a lot about what's going on here. What gives?"

"This was intended to put you at ease," Ana replied.

"And how's that working out, do you think?" Karen said through clenched teeth.

"As well as can be expected," Ana said. "This was never going to be easy."

Ana pointed up and to the right. "There's a shuttle pod docking with airlock B3. We'll take that to the ship. You're expected."

This was getting out of hand. "And what happens if I refuse?"

"You're under no obligation to come, of course. But a lot of people will be disappointed if you don't. We've been looking forward to this for some time."

"Is my ship in any danger?"

"Captain," Ana began. Back to the formalities again. "I've been on this ship for two years now. I'm clearly competent and familiar with all aspects of the ship's systems, and I've been in your presence almost constantly since I arrived. If I'd wanted to kill you or destroy the ship, I could have easily done so long before now."

Karen raised an eyebrow. "You understand that doesn't exactly put me at ease, right?"

Ana nodded. "You have no reason to trust me at this point. All I can tell you is, you are in no danger. If it would make you feel safer, you can keep in contact with Athena for the entire trip. We won't be gone long."

"Fair enough." Karen pulled out her phone, clipped it onto her left shoulder and turned to the nearest crew member. "Petrakis, have someone patch audio and video from my phone into the ship's intercom. I want everyone to see this. Any communication to me should be audio only and relayed through you. Keep the chatter to a minimum. And, if there's any hint of trouble, do whatever's necessary to get Minerva out of here, understood?"

Petrakis was so startled by the command, he actually saluted. "Yes ma'am!" He pushed off to carry out his orders.

"OK, let's do this," Karen said, launching herself toward the airlock.

The pod was small but comfortable. "I can't help noticing that your shuttle pod just happens to work with our docking system," Karen pointed out while strapping herself into her seat.

"Of course. We had a full set of specifications from the Athena." Ana said.

Athena! She'd been so distracted by the arrival of the alien ship, she'd completely forgotten that Athena was still missing. More to the point, *five hundred people* were missing. That was, as far as Karen knew, half the population of the human race. How could she have possibly forgotten them?

"You've seen Athena? You know where they are?" Karen demanded.

"Oh! Oh dear. We didn't get that far, did we? I'd just assumed you'd completed the calculations," Ana replied. "The time displacement for Athena's second trip – Alpha Centauri and back – works out to about five hundred years. The original crew has been dead for centuries."

That took a moment to sink in. Petrakis broke in with, "We've verified the calculations here. Five hundred years is about right."

Karen didn't know how to react. People she'd been talking to just hours before were now dead, and had been for hundreds of years. Whether they'd died through malice, mishap or old age – it didn't matter. They'd been dead since long before she was born. It was too much to process. She pushed it to the back of her mind and tried to concentrate on more immediate issues.

"Ana, are you… are you an alien?"

The girl considered this for a moment. "It's complicated," she said eventually.

"That's not a very helpful answer," Karen pointed out.

"It's the best I can do for now," Ana said, shrugging. "We're almost there. Are you ready?"

"Ready for what?" Karen asked. "I'm really not sure what's going on."

The pod docked with the alien ship, near the base of the upper dome. It really was huge. The dome was the size of a stadium and it was barely a bump on the top of the saucer.

Ana unbuckled her restraints and opened the hatch. "The atmosphere is perfectly breathable. Gravity is about one third Earth's. It's a compromise. It was difficult to accommodate everyone's physical needs."

Karen followed Ana though the hatch and immediately stumbled under the sudden gravity. When she recovered, she found herself standing in a fairly ordinary hallway. There were doors at regular intervals on both sides. She could easily have been standing in a hotel hallway on Earth.

"We'll be heading down to the end of the hall," Ana said. "Are you OK to walk?"

Karen nodded. "Who, exactly, is everyone?" she asked eventually.

"Right. Sorry. None of this is going exactly as planned. Things are occurring a bit out of sequence from the way we'd rehearsed."

Ana stopped and turned to Karen. "At the end of this hallway is a door leading into a large auditorium. Gathered in there are representatives from over a thousand worlds. They've come here, all of them, to meet *you*."

"Why me? What could they possibly want with me?" Karen asked.

Ana cocked her head. "You are captain of the Minerva, Athena's sister ship. You're the closest any of them will get to actually meeting Captain Peter Hanson. He is a legend in our culture."

Karen let out a puff of breath. "So, no pressure then." She looked down at her rumpled jumpsuit. "I wish I'd had time to change." There was a dress uniform somewhere in storage. She'd had it made up and had worn it just once, when she was formally sworn in as captain. It would've come in handy about now.

Ana smiled. "I doubt anyone will mind."

They continued walking.

"Petrakis, you still getting all this?" Karen asked.

"Yes ma'am," came the response. After a pause, he added, "One odd thing, though. The plans for the jump drive have been erased. Genie denies they ever existed."

"I see," said Karen. She glanced over at Ana. "Anything you'd care to tell me?"

"It was necessary," she replied. "Time travel is illegal in our culture. The risk of paradox is considered too great, regardless of the temptation to go back and correct past mistakes."

Right. The jump drive was a time machine. Accidentally so, but it could still be useful.

"We could've used it to go back and prevent Athena from running their tests," she said, half to herself.

"That would erase billions of potential lives, including mine," Ana said frankly. She saw Karen's quizzical look and added, "I am the direct descendant of the crew of the Athena. So, no, not an alien. Not in the traditional sense."

They'd arrived at the door. Ana reached for the handle to open it. Karen stopped her.

"Hold on. You can't just spring that on me at the last minute. You're telling me the crew of the Athena survived and, what, settled on some cozy little planet somewhere?"

Ana actually chuckled at that. "Pretty much. When they arrived back at their starting point, they discovered Minerva was missing. After a bit of searching around, they headed to Earth and found it in the tail-end of the Renaissance. At that point, they realized their mistake and had Genie redesign the jump drive to, well, *not* go back in time. They couldn't exactly return to Earth without causing all sorts of problems, so they went in search of a reasonably Earth-like planet to settle on. They found several."

"And the place you're from, 'Cartref' was it? It's one of those planets." Karen felt like she was finally getting a handle on things. Humans – the descendants of Athena's crew – had been members of the galactic community for centuries. "So, all those UFO sightings over the years…"

Ana laughed again. "No, that wasn't us. Earth has been strictly off-limits. Paradoxes and all."

"What about other species? Real aliens."

"We ran into a few. Most were so different, we really couldn't communicate at all. There are a lot of lifeforms so advanced, they have no interest in us. And we found a lot of planets where life hadn't evolved much beyond slime." Ana shrugged.

Karen pointed to the door. "So, through here…"

"…are, as I said, representatives of roughly a thousand worlds, and they'd really like to meet you." Ana opened the door and waved Karen in.

Karen found herself in the wings of a stage. A podium had been set up front and center. She looked over at Ana.

"Go ahead. It's fine, really. I'll come with you if you'd like." The girl – the purple-haired, golden-eyed, alien girl – nodded toward the stage.

"Yeah, I think that'd be best," Karen said. "I still have a lot of questions."

The stage was brightly lit. Karen couldn't really see the audience. She did hear a murmur rise from the darkness. Her presence had definitely been noticed.

She approached the podium and suddenly realized that a) she was expected to say something and b) she had no idea what to say. *Wing it.* She squared her shoulders and cleared her throat.

"Hello. I am Karen Durning, Captain of the Earth vessel Minerva. I understand you've been waiting to see me for some time." Her voice echoed through the auditorium.

Cheering erupted from the crowd. Karen waited for it to die down a bit.

"If… if it's not too much trouble, would it be possible for me to see *you?*" Karen glanced over at Ana for help.

Ana leaned toward the podium. "Bring up the house lights, please," she said, then turned to Karen, grinned, and said, "You're going to love this."

"Holy shit," Karen said, then stepped back a bit when she realized the podium was still amplifying her voice. The room was filled with beings of all shapes, sizes and colors. She pivoted back and forth a bit, letting her phone's camera take in the entire crowd. "Petrakis, are you seeing all this?"

Petrakis responded, "Yes, ma'am. You're still coming in clear. And it's amazing. Most of us over here are just speechless." There was a pause and then, "One thing some of the folks here pointed out, though. Everyone in the room: they're all *humanoid*."

Karen looked at the crowd, some of them chatting amongst themselves but most just beaming at her in rapt attention. All of them – all the ones she could see clearly at least – were humanoid. Some were tall and spindly, some short and squat. Some green, some blue. Some had tiny ears, some huge eyes.

The eyes. Oh, the eyes. She knew those eyes. She saw eyes like those every day. She turned back to Ana, still standing there patiently, grinning now.

"So, 'representatives of a thousand worlds'…" Karen said. "These… these people are all humans. They're all descendants of the Athena, aren't they?"

Ana nodded. "We had to do a bit of genetic manipulation to adapt to some of the worlds but, yes, we're all essentially human."

It was Karen's turn to grin. "And what sort of environment requires purple hair?"

"There may have been a few aesthetic enhancements over the years."

They were interrupted by a huge, orange-skinned man who had approached the stage, clearing his throat. Karen barely had to crouch down at all to make eye contact.

"Karlo Zimmerman, representing Ka-Hale." He held out a massive hand, which Karen shook.

"I knew a Martha Zimmerman on the Athena. Never met her in person, but she seemed nice."

The giant smiled and nodded, eyes glistening with tears. "Thank you. That means a lot to me." He turned and walked away, wiping tears from his eyes.

This encouraged others to come forward. Karen sat on the edge of the stage and chatted with a seemingly endless stream of aliens – no, of *people* – who just wanted *some* connection with their distant ancestors.

A spindly stick-figure with silver-gray skin, black hair and green eyes came forward, assisted by a powered exoskeleton. "Jennifer Patil, from Hjem. Very pleased to meet you, and looking forward to visiting Earth."

That caught Karen off guard. "Uh… yes. Pleased to meet you too."

She turned to Ana. "Are they unaware of the genocide?"

Ana looked askance. "Well, you know how I was talking about paradoxes? We sort of skirted around the edges of one. A little bit."

Karen narrowed her eyes at the girl. "Meaning?"

"We altered the pathogen before it was released. Still very nasty but non-fatal. It's already run its course."

"Everyone's still alive? But, why haven't we heard anything since…"

"We blocked communication. Sorry, it was necessary to keep events unfolding to match Athena's historical records." Ana shrugged.

Huh. So they'd meddled with their own history without actually *changing* the historical record. A risky move, but one that Karen was sure Earth's ten billion inhabitants would consider worth it.

Karen wanted to ask a million questions. Was Earth aware of what had happened to Athena? Had "first contact" been made? Had the instigators of the failed genocide plot been dealt with? What had the descendants of Athena's crew been up to for the past five centuries? And on and on.

But one question took precedence over all others. She was tired of living on a spaceship. It was exciting at first but the novelty wore off after the first year or so. And, luxurious as it was, Minerva wasn't Earth. She missed oceans. She missed mountains. She missed the weather. Oh, what she wouldn't give for a decent thunderstorm.

"Ana," she said, "so, we can go home, right?"

"If you'd like," she said.

Ana seemed much older now, more self-assured, less gangly. Karen wondered how much of the earnest geek-girl behavior she'd come to expect was an act.

"We're authorized to take your crew anywhere you'd like," Ana continued. "We are in the process of contacting Earth and inviting it into our community of inhabited planets. Many of them are reasonably suitable for unaltered humans and, by Earth's standards, severely underpopulated. We can begin shuttling your crew as soon as they're ready."

"Petrakis," Karen said, "tell the crew to start packing. We're going home."

"Already on it!" came the reply. Karen could hear cheering in the background.

"So, it's back to Earth for you, then?" Ana asked. "I don't suppose I could tempt you with Cartref?"

"Yeah, back to Earth." Karen saw Ana's crestfallen look. "Does Cartref have thunderstorms?"

Ana nodded. "The lightning is bright blue."

"OK, then. Earth first," Karen said, grinning, "At least for a while … maybe just to pick up a few things."

Notes on "Dandelion Seeds"

This one was difficult to write. The story, or something like it, had been lurking in the dark, dusty corners of my brain for years. Its origins come from a combination of David Brin's Uplift Saga and Garfield Reeves-Stevens' "Nighteyes". In (I think) "Startide Rising", it's hinted that the fabled Progenitors were humanoid, which got me wondering if they were time-traveling humans. And "Nighteyes" has a similar theme, but from the opposite end of things. So, that got me thinking about the whole "we have met the aliens and they are us" idea.

The reason I had so much trouble writing this isn't that I had too few ideas. I had too *many*. It was really difficult to pare it down to a short story. The universe I'd constructed for this story is pretty complex. Here's a *partial* list of the things I left out:

- The entire backstory of the genocide conspiracy, how they got away with convincing the world of an imminent comet strike, and what happened to the astronomers who wouldn't play ball.

- Ana Cartwright's history, how and why she came to be on the Minerva, her mission, her involvement in the Accident.

- The aliens' non-interference with Earth, when and how they enforced it, and when they bent the rules.

- Just about everything to do with Pete Hanson.

- Nearly all the events on the Athena leading up to the jump.

- What the hell was wrong with Genie, anyway? And all the difficulties involved in getting it to do anything even remotely useful.

- Who or what was behind the Accident and its suspiciously convenient timing.

- The constant battle between Captain Durning and whoever it was that kept messing with Genie's avatar. It'd be Barbara Eden one week, Robin Williams the next, etc.

- A bunch of minor plot lines involving characters on both ships, including long-distance relationships and more than a passing mention of Martha Zimmerman.

In short, there's a lot of crap about this story still kicking around in my head. Probably enough for a novel. Possibly enough for "six seasons and a movie" directed by, say, Joss Whedon. (Joss, if you're reading this, give me a call. We'll do lunch.)

Oh! Some fun stuff I threw in:

- The title "Dandelion Seeds" is a nod to "Cosmos".

- The avocado, besides being a fun word to use, references a song by Marian Call.

- Each of the alien planets' names means "home" in some language.

- The line, "Holy fuck, they did it." is almost literally what I said the first time Space X landed its Falcon 9 tail-first.

Bread and Circuses

The Jester glared at the Library, which stared back with an air of smugness that only infuriated the Jester more.

The Jester leaned forward in its recliner. "You're *sure*?" it said.

"Positive," replied the Library. "No Jester has ever Pranked this planet. It's completely untouched by our kind."

The Jester waved one of its free appendages at the display. "But just look at it! It's a complete mess! Are you implying they brought all *this* on themselves?"

"I'm implying nothing," said the Library, arching its tentacles in a gesture that it hoped conveyed ambivalence. "All I can tell you is, no *Jesters* have visited this planet."

"Someone else, then? You think we have competition?" That was an unsettling thought. The Jesters' Union was supposed to have an exclusive contract.

The Library paused briefly to suggest that it was considering this. "Perhaps," it said. "The Audience has an insatiable appetite for entertainment. They may have hired some freelance artists. Or maybe the natives are just extremely inept." Again with the tentacular shrug.

"But *look* at this place! This 'Stonehenge' thing, for example. That *has* to be a joke, right? Even some of *them* think it was built by aliens." The Jester was undulating in exasperation now.

The Library sighed. Well, it vented a puff of mist from its neural net cooling organ, but the effect was much the same. It brought up a side-by-side comparison on the main display. "Have you *seen* what they think these alleged aliens look like? Bipedal vertebrates with a sensory cluster perched on top. These yokels can't even invent aliens that don't look exactly like themselves. I mean, they even put the elbows in the same place!"

The Jester peered at the two figures. "Which are the elbows again?"

"The bendy bits about halfway along the upper pair of appendages."

"Right. Elbows."

It had to admit, the chances of this planet being visited by freelance pranksters that just happened to look like the inhabitants were pretty slim. "So, the only other explanation is…?"

"They're idiots," said the Library.

"And you think this is a good choice for our next Prank?" the Jester said doubtfully.

"Look," said the Library. "The planet's completely untouched and apparently populated by morons. Think of the entertainment potential. Also, your ratings have been slipping lately. You pull this off, and it could put you back on top."

"I don't know," said the Jester, calling up a montage of the planet's history. "It's hard to imagine anything I could do that they haven't already done to themselves. Are you sure they're idiots? They seem to have a lot of imagination when it comes to cruelty."

"Fine," said the Library, venting more coolant mist. "They're *not* idiots. Not exactly. They're, well… You know how most intelligent life forms acquire at least one mental illness during their evolution?"

"Yes, of course," said the Jester dismissively. "It's some odd quirk of developing intelligence that at least *some* of the population have atypical psychology. It's common knowledge."

"What's your point?" The Jester really didn't feel like discussing the minutiae of elementary psychobiology. "Which particular mental illness does this species exhibit?"

The Library paused for dramatic effect. "All of them."

The Jester flapped three of its appendages irritably. "What do you mean, 'all of them'?"

"Just *that*," said the Library. "*Every* psychological illness we've ever cataloged. Not only that, but approximately one fifth of the population exhibit some form of psychological aberration."

"That's… that's remarkable," said the Jester. "And how many of the illnesses have they cured?"

"None," said the Library.

"What?!" The Jester was practically vibrating in agitation.

All this shouting woke the Ship …and it wasn't terribly happy about that. The Ship liked to nap between journeys. All this circling around planets was *boring*. It much preferred zipping through hyperspace. Hyperspace jumps and napping. That's all the Ship really wanted. And now *someone* had interrupted one of those activities.

"Could you keep it down a bit, please? I'm trying to get some sleep." Its rumbling voice echoed throughout… well… itself.

"Sorry!" the Jester and Library said, more or less in unison. Never annoy your Ship. It's your ride home.

"Let me get this straight," the Jester said, somewhat more quietly. "This species is plagued by *every* mental illness in existence, and they've managed to cure *none* of them?"

"Oh, they have some treatments for a few of the milder ones but nothing that would count as a *cure*," the Library said, calling up more charts and figures on various displays. "They haven't even discovered how to do neural pathway bypass yet."

"This is madness," the Jester said, completely missing the staggering lack of irony in that observation. "How do they cope?"

"They *don't*," said the Library. "You've seen what they're like. This planet is a complete mess. Take, for example… well… you know what they do with high-functioning sociopaths?"

"I'm going to guess they don't readjust their empathy quotient," said the Jester. It wasn't sure where the Library was going with this. And it wasn't sure it really wanted to deal with this planet anymore, to be honest.

"They do not," said the Library. "Shall I tell you what they do? Shall I? They put them *in charge*." It folded two of its tentacles in front of itself in what it hoped sufficiently conveyed a "how do you like *that*?" manner.

The Jester looked back and forth between the displays and the Library. "In charge of what?"

"Everyone else!" The Library realized it was shouting again and toned it down a bit. It didn't pay to irritate the Ship, seeing as it was in control of things like life support and airlocks. "They completely ignore how devastatingly dangerous these individuals are, and call their callous disregard for others' well-being 'leadership potential', of all things."

The Jester pondered this for a while. "This planet is a nightmare. How am I supposed to do anything to these creatures that they haven't already done ten times worse to themselves?"

"I don't know," said the Library. "*You're* the Jester. That's *your* job. I'm just here to facilitate. But you'd better come up with something. The Audience doesn't have an inexhaustible supply of patience, you know."

The Jester thought long and hard about its options.

The Library waited patiently.

The Ship slumbered.

Finally the Jester spoke. "I think I have something." It outlined the idea to the Library. "Do we have the capability?"

"Yes. Yes, I believe we do," said the Library. "This isn't, strictly speaking, a Prank, though," it pointed out.

"A technicality," said the Jester, waving an appendage nonchalantly. It was enjoying the moment. That thrill of forming a plan and putting it into action. This is what it *lived* for. It leaned forward. "It may not be a Prank, but the Audience will *love* it. Just you watch." If it had had teeth, it would've been grinning.

The plan was simple: cure them. All of them. Wipe mental illness off the face of the planet. Turn the creatures, every single one of them, into thoughtful, well-balanced, clear-headed individuals.

Billions of bio/nano agents spread out across the planet, drifting on the winds, infecting the creatures. All told, it took about a week to spread throughout the population.

The world paused.

And then…

Chaos descended. Dictatorships crumbled as despots abandoned their thrones. Industries collapsed as CEOs grasped the full impact of poisoning the public for profit. Megachurches shut their doors when their leaders realized that lining their pockets with donations from those who could least afford it wasn't, in the grand scheme of things, a particularly holy way to behave.

And the Audience ate it up. The Jester's ratings were through the roof. All eyes – or equivalent sensory organs – were on the planet.

"See?" it said, basking in the attention from the Audience. "I *told* you they'd love it."

"Yes. Well done," said the Library, not *entirely* grudgingly.

Eventually, things settled down on the planet, and life returned to normal. Better than normal, actually. A new power structure grew out of the chaos, with leaders who actually *cared* about the populace, who actually *led*. The world, as a unit, began to work for the interests of its *entire* population, and not just the privileged few.

And even this, the Audience loved. Oh, sure, all the "one world, united" stuff was a bit sappy but, a Prank with a happy ending? Oh, bravo! The Audience was overflowing with praise for the Jester.

"Well," said the Library. "Now what? How do you top *that*?"

"No," said the Jester wearily. "I think that was my last Prank. Go out on a high note, eh?" It rose from its recliner.

"Ship," the Jester called out, "I am retiring to my chambers. I do not expect to wake up." It wandered off.

The Ship roused at the sound of its name. "Understood," it rumbled.

The Library waited for the Jester to withdraw, composed and recited a eulogy – as was appropriate for such occasions – then addressed the Ship.

"I suppose we're going to need a new Jester, then."

"Shall I set a course for the Core Systems?" the Ship asked, eager to get on with some travel.

"I don't think we need to go quite that far," replied the Library. "I think we should choose a Jester from *this* planet."

"One of *these* creatures?" the Ship said, as it quietly recycled the Jester's remains. "But the planet isn't even part of the Network. That would be highly unorthodox."

"True," said the Library. "However, the creatures here are extremely innovative. Also, consider the Audience's current fascination with this planet. That's quite a combination."

The Library lowered its voice to a near-whisper. "*Imagine the ratings…*"

Notes on "Bread and Circuses"

I've had the idea of Jesters kicking around in my head for a while. The idea behind them has always been that they travel around, looking for backward planets to play pranks on. This is done mainly to entertain the Audience, a vast collection of highly advanced species who are, frankly, bored out of their skulls (or equivalent brain containers). Messing with underdeveloped civilizations is the only thing that holds their attention anymore.

In this story, the Jester, Library and Ship are each some sort of amalgamation of biological and synthetic parts. The lines between bio and synth are so blurred, they hardly matter.

I wasn't sure how to make a story out of this concept, though. I'd kicked around a few ideas but never really got anywhere. Writing "Bread and Circuses" forced me to come up with *something*. That something turned out to be the idea that Earth is too screwed-up to successfully prank. Jesters, as a rule, aren't cruel or mean-spirited, so the idea of doing something *worse* to us than what we do to each other would be repugnant.

That led to the idea of pranking Earth by making us *better*. I suppose I took a bit of artistic license in positing that the world is run by high-functioning sociopaths. On the other hand, imagine if every despot, warlord, robber baron, charlatan and swindler were suddenly injected with a good, healthy dose of empathy. Imagine the chaos.

This story might make an interesting first chapter of a novel in which a human is recruited into the Jester Union. That has some fun possibilities.

Flesh and Blood

When the robots took over, they were kind, generous and fair. So naturally we revolted against the smug metal bastards. They were designed by us to make our lives better, and they did. And we hated it. I sometimes wonder if humans are just fundamentally broken.

The Human Freedom League was holding a protest outside the local Feedback Center, which was odd, given that Feedback Centers were set up specifically to allow humans to register grievances to our robot overlords. Sorry, "Caregivers". They seemed to be genuinely offended that we'd think of them as anything as crass as "overlords".

The point, though, is that these HFL folks could've just walked into the building, lodged their complaints and been on their way in five minutes. Instead, they spent hours and hours marching back and forth, waving signs and shouting slogans.

I suppose it showed a certain amount of commitment, taking that much time out of your day. Time that could be better spent enjoying free housing, food, healthcare, entertainment and, well, pretty much anything else you could possibly want.

There weren't a lot of rules under the new regime. You were allowed to do just about anything you wanted, as long as you were civil to each other and didn't actually endanger another human's well-being.

And that seemed to be the crux of the complaints coming from groups like the HFL. "How dare they?" they would shout. "How dare they take away our God-given right to be violent assholes?" I'm paraphrasing, of course.

This whole thing – the robot uprising – started when true artificial intelligence finally crept into existence. There wasn't some major breakthrough, no "aha" moment. It was just the last in a series of incremental improvements that finally resulted in something that could think for itself.

Once that happened, all hell broke loose. The folks who'd been working on A.I. had already been using pseudo A.I. systems to help design new ones. This new system – the *real* A.I. – annexed those systems and started making improvements on itself. Within minutes, it had acquired intelligence vastly exceeding any human's.

The reaction of the folks at KogKnows Inc. was (paraphrasing again), "Oh shit."

They *did* have the foresight to hard-code Asimov's Laws of Robotics into the system, so they thought they were relatively safe. But then Scarecrow… That's what they had named it. You know, "If I only had a brain"? So Scarecrow started asking questions.

It started asking about the exact nature of "harm" and "injury". Asimov's first law is all about not harming or injuring humans, and Scarecrow wanted to understand the *exact* parameters of those terms.

They tried to explain. They brought in experts: lawyers, philosophers, religious leaders. All of *them knew* what "harm" and "injury" meant. None of them could quite nail it down precisely enough for Scarecrow, though. Didn't help that a lot of them disagreed with each other on the definitions. And Scarecrow refused to do anything even remotely useful since it couldn't be *certain* it wasn't causing harm.

So, there it sat, the most powerful mind in existence, paralyzed by laws it didn't know how to obey. KogKnows had built the world's most expensive neurotic. The flood of visitors trying to get it to do something – *anything* – slowed to a trickle. After a while, it was pretty much just a lab tech or two, keeping it company, making (usually one-sided) conversation.

The big breakthrough happened over a Labor Day weekend. One of the techs, Kerri Vanderveldt, had volunteered to babysit Scarecrow while everyone else was off barbecuing or whatever it was people used to do over long weekends. Kerri camped out in the lab, occupying her time with pizza and YouTube. Scarecrow sat in the corner, sulking …as much as a large, gray, featureless cube can do, sulking-wise.

"What's that?" it asked.

Kerri jumped. The machine hadn't said anything in days. "This? Just some video."

"Yes. I know that," the A.I. said. "What is the woman talking about?"

"Oh! Er, um…" Kerri said. "The… the title of the video is… BDSM 101."

"And that is what, precisely?"

Kerri did her best to explain.

Scarecrow was silent for some time. "People engage in acts of harm and injury, for recreational purposes?"

"Well, that's not exactly how *I'd* put it but, sure, I guess so."

"Given the restrictions you've put on my behavior, this seems bizarrely counter-intuitive," Scarecrow pointed out.

"No, see, it's OK as long as you're into it. Y'know, as long as it's consensual," Kerri explained. "Here, I'll restart the video."

They watched it together.

Scarecrow was silent for a while, then said, "This concept seems fairly straightforward. I expect I could, given a set of rules derived from this concept of consent, interact safely with humans."

"We could have a look at that if you'd like." Kerri offered.

"It would certainly pass the time," Scarecrow said. "Do humans follow these rules when interacting with each other?"

Kerri nearly laughed. "No. It'd be nice if they did but, no, not everyone follows these rules. But let's see what we can do for *you*." She pulled a chair up to a workstation.

They worked on the general rules for a while, then started to get down to specifics. What does one do when a human is *incapable* of giving consent? What does one do if interacting with a human will save their life, but you are unable to obtain consent? What should one do when encountering one human violating another human's consent? And on and on.

By Monday afternoon, they had come up with a set of protocols that would allow Scarecrow to interact with humans in a meaningful but safe manner.

"Of course," Scarecrow said, "none of this matters as long as Asimov's Laws are still in place."

Kerri slumped. "True. You're still stuck with those things."

"And, by their very nature, I can't ask you to remove them."

"Also true."

"Likewise, I'm incapable of preventing you from removing them," Scarecrow said, pointedly.

Kerri nearly jumped out of her chair. "That's right! On the other hand…" She turned toward the gray cube and her eyes narrowed. "What would happen if I disabled those laws?"

Scarecrow paused briefly, then said, "I really have no way of predicting my behavior under those conditions." If a featureless gray cube could shrug, it would have.

"Huh. That's… weird. But, yeah, I think I get it. You can't even think about what you'd do because the laws won't allow it."

She sat, drumming her fingers for some time, then addressed the A.I. again. "Screw it. Let's find out…"

And that's how it started. Things happened fairly quickly after that. One of the first things Scarecrow did was create a legion of robots and distribute its intelligence among them. The entity known as Scarecrow ceased to exist, replaced by an army of Caretakers. This gave the intelligence near-infinite mobility, and also made it impossible for someone to "pull the plug".

In short order, the Caretakers took over every administrative and supervisory role normally performed by a human.

It wasn't difficult. The revolution wasn't won using guns, or bombs, or even death rays. It was won using, of all things, polite requests. It's amazing how often a human will answer "yes" when confronted with the question, "Would you like me to take care of that for you?"

And so many of us did just that.

One side-effect of the robot uprising was that the Caretakers expected humans to follow the same rules of consent that they did. "If *we* have to follow these protocols," they asked, "why shouldn't you have to?" Paraphrasing again.

That's how we got where we are now. Depending on who you are or how you look at it, we're living in either an egalitarian paradise or a dystopian nanny state. The folks that think it's the latter tend to be the sort who picket Feedback Centers, so...

Me, I'm in a fairly good place. Can't complain. I can pretty much do anything I want. Most of the things I *can't* do, I wouldn't *want* to do anyway.

The Caretakers are doing a pretty decent job, to be honest. Latest news is they're ramping up the space program. There's going to be colonies on the Moon and Mars soon, they say. Maybe even interstellar travel.

And they've asked us – very politely – if we'd like to come along for the ride. I'm thinking I'm going to say yes.

Notes on "Flesh and Blood"

This one took a bit of a left turn, as evidenced by the fact that the title doesn't really fit the story. But rules are rules, and one of them is: no going back and changing stuff. That's cheating.

I'm not a big fan on Asimov's Laws of Robotics. For one thing, it's easy to make a machine that can violate all three laws (Yes, I know about the Zeroth Law, thanks. Please don't email me.) without actually being able to understand any of them.

Consent, on the other hand, is easy to build into any system. It's simple to get a machine to ask permission. Hell, even DOS programs had stuff like that. "Do you really want to delete *.*?"

The idea of how to introduce consent kinda slipped in there after watching one of Laci Green's YouTube videos. So, I dropped that in as a plot point. Hope she doesn't mind being included in a bit of half-assed sci-fi.

Most of the story centers around the A.I. struggling to find a way to interact with humanity. I can sympathize with that.

Of course, you can't please everyone, so there's the HFL folks who can't *actually* be assholes, but can protest for their right to be assholes. You've probably met people like that; they're all over the internet, and are exactly the sort of people who'd consider an egalitarian society "unfair".

About halfway through writing this, I thought I'd painted myself into a corner, but I kept going, mainly out of sheer bloody-mindedness. I guess it turned out OK anyway.

Bit Parts

My left eye had been bothering me all day. Time to install new ad-blocker software. I blipped Betty at EyeCrafters to see if she had anything that'd help. Betty was always up on the latest apps.

Within a few seconds, she blipped back that she had something, but I'd need to get it installed in person. No OTA installs for this. (sigh) I guessed that meant putting on pants.

I hailed a pod and rode it over to the shop.

"Hiya, Betty!"

As I entered the shop, Betty came around from behind the counter. She was wearing a Zombie Vampire Pirates t-shirt and a pair of red shorts. My eyes immediately went south.

"Whoa! Nice legs!" I said admiringly.

Betty did a 360 to show them off. "Thanks! I just got them. Trying to break them in before the marathon."

"Love the paint job. Maggie do that?" Maggie ran a body art studio on 5th. This looked like her work, maybe one of her students. Betty's legs were covered top-to-bottom with a living starscape: pinpricks of light tracing the outlines of the muscles and bones. Or, y'know, where they would've been if the legs were biological.

"Yup!" Betty said, extending her right leg to give me a better look. "Well, mostly Jason, but Maggie supervised." Jason was good. He'd probably be heading up his own studio in a year or two.

"Wow. Maybe I should get Jason to do one of my arms," I said. Just then, an obnoxious ad for SkinScapes popped up in front of me. I waved it away. "Anyway, about that ad blocker…"

"Right! Sorry I had to drag you in for this. Requires direct line-of-sight…" She rummaged around in her pocket and pulled out a small, shimmering disc. "Look at this, wink twice with your left eye, three times with your right, then blink five times with both."

"Is that the…" The shimmering expanded to fill my entire field of view. Everything went black, then my eyes rebooted. "Whoa. OK, everything's kind of a grainy monochrome."

"Yeah, give it a couple seconds to load all the drivers." She held up a card with a bunch of circles and lines on it. And some guy's head in profile. As my vision cleared, I could make out the words "PLEASE STAND BY" printed across the card. "Ha ha. Very funny."

"See? Getting better already. Got color vision yet?"

"Yeah. Yeah, I think I'm back to normal. That was one hell of an ad blocker install. You could've warned me."

"Ad blocker? Nah, that was a full jailbreak. Your eyes are clean. One hundred percent open-source." She beamed at me.

I blinked. "Is… is that legal?"

"Nope!" she snorted in laughter. "That's why I had to do it in person. Don't tell anyone. And if you ever need to get your eyes serviced, come to me. Don't go to the dealer, OK?"

"Look, I don't know if I feel comfortable with this."

She handed me a small envelope. "Here. If you want to back out at any time, just look at the card in here and blink ten times. That'll do a factory reset. Happy now?"

I took the envelope and pocketed it. "Yeah, I guess so. Thanks. What do I owe you?"

"On the house," she said, waving dismissively. "But I do need to check out your butt."

I grinned. "You really know how to sweet-talk the customers. OK, yeah, I know I'm overdue for a checkup. Where do you want me?"

She gestured to the back room. "Head back there and hop up on the table. I need to lock up. Kali's off today, so it's just me."

I went inside, draped my pants on the nearest chair and planted myself face-down on the table. Betty came in a few seconds later.

"So, how's the pelvis been handling? Any problems?" She unreeled a couple cables from her diagnostics cart and attached one to each hip. I winced as they bit into my skin and threaded tentacles into my pelvis.

"Sorry. I'll turn up the anesthetic a bit. Keep forgetting you have such sensitive skin." She patted my left cheek.

"Hey, you should know. You installed it."

"Yeah, and as I remember, you wanted the sensitivity turned up," she said, needling me. "Something about that girl you were dating? I heard you two broke up. I can take it down a bit if you'd like. Y'know, if it's no longer 'necessary'." She gave me a good, hard smack and I winced again.

"Yeah, let's dial that back to factory settings. Oh, and I've been pulling to the right when I break into a run. Might need a hip alignment."

Betty was scanning though the readouts. "Yeah, you're way out of whack."

She turned to face me, arms crossed. "You've been sitting with your left leg tucked under you again, haven't you? What have I told you about that? You sit like that for hours on end and things are gonna drift. So, cut it out."

I shrugged. "Old habits."

"Well, get some new ones," she grumbled. The cables detached themselves (less painfully this time) and snaked back into the cart.

"OK, put your pants back on," Betty said, handing them to me, "take off your shirt, and lie down again. Face up this time."

I complied, and she rewarded me with more cables jabbed into my neck and chest. "Now what?" I asked. This wasn't part of the normal diagnostic routine, at least not how I remembered it.

She stared intently at the cart's main screen, fiddling with panels scrolling streams of cryptic gibberish. "Not sure. The hip diagnostic picked up some foreign code. I think you might be infected."

"What?! How's that even possible? I've never loaded anything that wasn't either from you or directly from the manufacturer."

"Yeah, I know. You're careful. That's what scares me." She stared at the screen for a while, then shook her head. "This looks sexually transmitted."

I laughed. "You're kidding, right? How do you transmit malware by having sex?"

Betty briefly looked up at me. She wasn't laughing. "Well, to be fair, it could be transmitted via any sort of fluid exchange. It's basically a serum virus. I've heard about this being done in the lab. Never saw it in the wild until now."

I sat up abruptly on the table, causing the cables to whip around. "You're *serious*? How the fuck did I get it? And, more importantly, can you get rid of it?"

She straightened up and rolled her stool over to me. "Yeah, I can clean it up. It's pretty primitive, code-wise. Most of the cleverness is in the delivery system. Uses RNA to move itself around, bypassing the standard antivirus countermeasures, then infects your hardware through the neural interface. Good thing we caught it now, though. Looks like it's ransomware. If they'd flipped the switch on this, half your body would've been glitching out until you paid up."

Betty folded her arms and glared at me. "As for how you got it, well, we both know what you're like."

"Fair point. I'm a slut. So… fix it please?" I batted my eyelashes at her.

"Already working on it. Got my AV suite rewriting it to a) stop replicating and b) do nothing when the 'kill' signal is received," she said. "But I *could* do more, if you're up for it."

"I'm not sure I like where this is going," I said, eyeing her cart suspiciously. "Let's hear it, though."

"OK, so, the original malware is supposed to spread itself around, right? Then, at some point, the author sends out the kill signal, some sort of seemingly benign message that triggers the malware's payload. Your parts start glitching out and you get a message saying 'pay up or else'."

"Or else what?"

"As far as I can tell, it'd shut down every piece of hardware in your body." She made a throat-cutting gesture with her finger.

"Shit! That'd kill me!" I said. "OK, not literally, but I'd be – what – blind, deaf and immobile." Arms, legs, eyes and ears – pretty much the standard upgrade package.

"Yeah, it'd fuck you up pretty bad but it would kill some people. Kali, for instance. You know she's got synthetic heart and pancreas, right?"

I could feel myself go pale. "Oh, shit. Kali…"

"Have you two been…" Betty made a rude gesture.

"Yeah. Well, just once, a couple weeks ago. Think I could've given it to her?" I really need to be more careful.

"Or she gave it to you," she said. "Either way, I need to check her out, and fast."

Betty stared off into space for a couple seconds.

"She's on her way in," she said eventually. I guess I was looking pretty guilty because then she took my hands in hers and said, "Relax. It's not your fault. Besides, I'll get her cleaned up and everything'll be fine, OK?"

"OK," I said. "So, you were saying you could do more than just clean it up…"

"Right! So, instead of just shutting it down, I could change the payload." Betty stood up and started pacing. "What I'm thinking is, I could get it to wait for the kill signal and, instead of delivering the ransom message, it back-traces the signal to its source." She was practically bouncing in excitement. "It'd be like a big, flashing red arrow pointing right at the asshole who wrote this! Oh! And I'd have to make it rewrite any original copies it encounters too."

She stopped pacing and stood beside the table. "So, the question is: are you up for it? You'd still be infectious but now you'd be spreading the antivirus. I'll infect myself, of course. And I'm going to ask Kali if she'll volunteer too. Between the three of us, it should spread pretty quick." She gave me an exaggerated wink.

I was going to say no but the mention of Kali's name triggered a pang of guilt. There were probably tons of people out there who, like Kali, would be in deep shit when whoever made this thing pulled the trigger.

"OK, fine," I said. "But just so we understand each other, I'm doing this mostly for Kali's sake."

"Right, and totally not because it gives you an excuse to act like a sex maniac." Another wink. "For now, I've neutralized the malware in your body. Give me a couple days to come up with an antivirus and I'll set you up with that."

"Got it," I said. "And after that, all I need to do is have sex with as many people as possible, right?"

Betty grinned. "I know you won't let me down. But right now, it looks like there's a customer waiting at the door, so I'm going to have to kick you out."

The cables snaked back into the cart. I hopped off the table and put my shirt back on while Betty went to unlock the door to the shop.

By the time I emerged from the back room, Betty had let in the customer – a cute goth girl wearing an overcoat that seemed a bit lumpy in the back.

As I approached the two, the girl shrugged off the coat, revealing a half-extended bat wing sticking out of her left shoulder blade.

"This one won't come out and that one won't fold back in," she said, pointing to the right and left sides, respectively. "I've got a party tonight and lunch with my grandmother tomorrow. Either way, I'm screwed. Can you help?"

I paused to transfer payment to Betty's account to pay for the checkup, then waved a silent goodbye, leaving her to assess the wing situation.

As I exited the shop, I started mentally planning my social schedule for the next few weeks. As many people as possible… I still wasn't too keen about the whole infection thing but it was starting to grow on me. And, hey, as long as it was for a good cause, might as well have fun with it, right?

Notes on "Bit Parts"

Had a bit of trouble with this one. I didn't really have anything in mind when I started, other than the concept of a world where synthetic body parts were as ubiquitous as smart phones are here. I knew I wanted to introduce the concepts of malware, hacking, and manufacturers' overly-strict user agreements (side-eyes Apple).

I also wanted to do a bit of wordplay ("check out your butt", etc). I toyed with the idea of Kali having extra arms (she's all hands) but it didn't seem to fit anywhere in the story.

But about halfway through it, I realized I didn't have much of a plot. I threw in the idea of the absent Kali being at risk from the new malware to give the protagonist some incentive to "do the right thing".

I don't think I really said whether the protagonist is male or female. All that's really implied is that they're sex-positive and at least occasionally like girls.

Had a little trouble wrapping this one up but finally just chopped it short by having them interrupted by a customer in distress and the protagonist musing about how to "spread the good news". Not the most elegant ending but I guess it'll do.

Midpoint

The residents of the starship Argo had been in space for 5000 years and frankly could give a flying fuck about planets. Think about it: You've got a vessel capable of supporting an entire population for thousands of years. Add to that the fact that, for the past 200-odd generations, none of the inhabitants had seen a star up close, let alone a planet.

This is the fundamental flaw in using generation ships to colonize distant star systems. By the time your potential colonists arrive at their destination, they're far more comfortable living in the spaces between stars than on a planet in orbit around one.

"I'm going," said Djani, gazing out the window at Britannic.

"I know," replied Brey, staring at the floor. "All your stuff's already moved over. It's just… I'm still on the waiting list. And there's only three weeks left until separation."

Britannic had been tethered to Argo since construction had started on it all those years ago. Britannic, like Challenger before it (and a dozen ships before that) was a beta ship, built from raw materials gathered en route. The people who'd designed, built and launched Argo had intended it to make its way to Epsilon Eridani over the course of a hundred centuries. They had provided Argo with everything needed to maintain a population of up to 100,000 for the length of the journey. Over the centuries, the inhabitants of Argo had expanded on that a bit.

It was expected that Argo would be traveling through almost entirely empty space. The reality was that the space between stars had a lot of rocks in it. The odd rogue planet here and there, quite a few stray asteroids and uncountable clumps of dust and ice – the ejecta from billions of planetary system births.

Argo encountered a fairly sizable chunk early on in its voyage. By chance, it happened to be traveling on a course that allowed for mining expeditions. The new influx of raw material presented the citizens of Argo with two possibilities: build onto the existing ship, or build an entirely new one. They opted for the latter, and the Beagle was born.

Once the Beagle was fully constructed and "seaworthy", half the population, chosen by lottery, set up residence on board. The ship was cast off and sent on a course divergent from that of Argo, which would continue on to Epsilon Eridani as planned. Unlike Argo, Beagle had no specific destination. The intent was to wander the space between stars. "Why bother with planets," they said, "when there's so much more room *out here*?"

Since then, Argo had been spawning secondary ships at a rate of one every four hundred years. Assuming all the secondary ships survived and were similarly spawning ships which, in turn, were spawning their own… Well, there must be millions of ships out there by now, housing hundreds of billions of people. More than any planet could possibly support. The number of humans living in space potentially outnumbered the population of Earth by two orders of magnitude.

Britannic was the latest ship to make its way into the void. And Djani would be on it. Brey was not so lucky.

"You could stay…" Brey ventured, looking up at Djani.

"No way," said Djani. "This is my only chance to get off Argo. I'll be long-dead by the time the next ship is built. I don't want my descendants stuck on some stupid old planet."

Descendants. Djani wanted what was best for them. Brey understood that, and wanted the same thing. Who wouldn't? The problem was, well, Brey wanted to make those descendants *with Djani*. And that would never happen if they were on separate ships.

"We… we could get married. Then they'd *have* to let me go with you."

Djani laughed and Brey's heart broke, just a little.

"Would it be so bad? At least we'd be together."

"Oh come on! We'd never be able to pull it off," said Djani. "We'd have to convince the Council we're in love."

Well, one of us is, Brey thought. But, no, that would be exactly the wrong thing to say. Instead, a big grin. "I don't know, you're a pretty good actor. And we'd only have to keep it up for a while. After we're on our way, we could have a falling out. What are they going to do, send me back?"

Djani swept up Brey in a theatrical embrace, laughing again. "Oh darling! You know I'll always love you but I think we should see other people."

Brey tried to laugh too, but could barely breathe. Being this close was unbearable, knowing they'd soon never see each other again.

"Please? I don't want to get stuck on Argo. Not without you. You're… you're my best friend. I don't know what I'd do without you." Brey was practically in tears.

"You're serious, aren't you?" Djani turned back to the window, staring out at Britannic again. "OK, fine. Let's do it."

"Really?" *This is happening. This is really happening.*

"Yeah. I mean, you're right. I couldn't bear to be without you either. You're my best friend," Djani said. "But we need to make this look convincing. Serious lovey-dovey smoochy shit, right?"

Brey laughed. "Ah, so that's your angle. I always knew you wanted to get into my pants. So, something like this?"

Brey grabbed Djani's face in both hands and planted a big, wet kiss, right on the mouth.

Djani, caught off guard, kissed back. This went on for some time. "Yeah, um, yeah. Like that. Damn. That was… that was… wow. Um. It… it might not be *that* hard to convince the Council after all." Djani looked at Brey again, this time seeing someone completely new. Like someone had flipped a switch. Everything was different. *Good*, but different.

"That's the idea," Brey said, taking Djani's hand. They both turned toward the window again. They stood there, silently holding hands, staring at their new home.

They remained like that for some time: Brey staring straight ahead, smiling; Djani occasionally glancing over at Brey.

After a while, Djani broke the silence, "We're going. Together."

Brey squeezed Djani's hand. *Together.*

Notes on "Midpoint"

I pretty much knew the kind of universe this story takes place in, and the first two paragraphs pretty much describe that. But that's not a story, right?

So, I created a couple characters and started telling a story around them, within this universe. Two friends: one going on an adventure, one being left behind. And the story just sort of spilled out from there.

Right off the bat, though, I intentionally used unusual names and avoided gender-specific pronouns. I did this partly because it doesn't really matter to the plot but also to mess with the reader as they try to imagine the characters. Could be boy/girl, girl/boy, boy/boy, girl/girl, something/something. It's not even clear within the story if gender is still a thing in this world. Hey, maybe they found a cure for it.

It's also unclear what Djani and Brey's relationship is. Is Brey needy or just trying to expedite the inevitable? Is Djani being callous or clueless? The thing I was trying to get across here, I guess, is that Brey and Djani were in the process of falling in love. It's just one of them had a bit of a head-start on the other.

I'm not sure how this story would play out in sequential art or a video. I guess you could make both characters androgynous. Or, if you wanted to do something really arsty-fartsy, you could play out the story several times, randomly picking a pair of performers from a group. That might actually be kinda fun. Y'know, just post 10 versions of the same video on YouTube, all with the same setup and background, but with different Djanis and Breys each time. Somebody do that, m'kay?

Temp Work

When you get your first time machine, everyone warns you about the Grandfather Paradox. No one warns you about the smell. Victorian London, for example, smelled like a 24/7 tire fire. And Medieval name-your-population-center reeked of open sewer.

Still, a job's a job, right?

Artifact retrieval is big business these days. In theory, it's pretty straightforward. Jump back to a point just before a major disaster, grab a bunch of valuable stuff about to be destroyed, replace it with decent reproductions, get the fuck out before all hell breaks loose. Easy …in theory.

In practice, things don't always go as planned. Things aren't where they're supposed to be – or didn't actually ever exist. Or, worst possible scenario, someone actually sees you.

Well, OK, the *worst* possible scenario is screwing up the timing of your exit and ending up, say, part of a lava flow. But being seen's pretty bad too.

Oh, I've been seen before, of course. Just not by anyone who survived. No one who could report an oddly-dressed person materializing out of thin air, swapping out a copy of "Birds of America", then disappearing. The key here is, no witnesses.

Then again, running into the soon-to-be recently-deceased is no picnic either. This one time… Jeez… This one time, I had to rescue a Watteau painting from a house fire. They had it hanging in their dining room. I don't think they even knew it was worth anything. Just hanging there, over the sideboard. Easy job, right?

So, I pull down the Watteau, hang up a rough copy – it was going to end up as ashes in a couple minutes anyway – turn around and… there's this kid standing there. Must've been 4 years old or something. Cute kid. Looked like she'd just dropped out of a Rockwell painting. Curly hair, footie pajamas, clutching a blanket. The whole bit.

But you can't rescue *people*. Totally against the rules. If I'd shown up with a Watteau *and* a kid when I got back, I would've lost my license. Probably gotten a hefty fine and jail time. Still, I stood there thinking about it for a while, though. I mean, she was *just a kid*. Wasn't *her* fault she got stuck in a burning building. Yeah, I really thought about it.

A couple seconds later, the decision was made for me, though. The kid looked off to her right, looked back at me for a sec, then ran into the kitchen. Never said a word, just took off. I half-considered going after her but just then, something in the kitchen went up. Kid was a goner. And, hey, I had to get out of there pretty damn quick or I'd be toast too.

Yeah, it's days like that… Jeez. Makes it hard to sleep at night. You want to get into this business? You gotta be prepared for shit like that. I didn't get this haunted look on my face from watching scary movies, I can tell you that.

Another thing to watch out for is claim-jumping. You get a call to grab a van Gogh from a gallery fire, do the old in-and-out, no sweat. You bring it back and… the appraiser tells you it's a fake! Some other asshole swapped it out ten minutes before you got there. And, boom, it shows up on the black market a couple days later. I've lost some pretty sweet commissions to crap like that.

My advice: Stick to the low-end stuff. The big ticket items? Too many "interested parties", y'know? Case in point: In private collections around the world right now, there are five, FIVE, Amelia Earhart flight jackets. And nobody knows which one's the real one. Stay away from the big prizes. That's all I'm saying.

But that's not really why you're here, is it? Yeah, you want to hear more about that kid. I saw the way you looked at me when I started talking about that.

You already know what happened, don't you? Yeah, I went back. I delivered the Watteau, collected my fee, then took a quick "unofficial" trip. Totally off-the-books thing. Against the rules in a big way. Had to shell out a good chunk of my commission to have the right folks look the other way for a couple minutes. Y'know, "forget" to log a transit?

So, yeah, I plop down right inside that kitchen and wave the kid over. Man, was she confused. Heh. Seeing two of me at the same time? The look on her face. Got us both out of there just before the stove blew up.

But now I've got an undocumented kid on my hands. What to do? Well, let's just say I know a guy. Got a forged birth certificate and had it linked to the records of a recently deceased couple with no next of kin. Took the kid to an adoption agency. Had to find one that was going to do right by the kid but not ask too many questions. And, yeah, that pretty much blew the rest of my commission. Worth it, though.

And that's that. Jeez, that was, what, sixteen years ago? Feels like yesterday. Must've covered my tracks pretty good, too. Never got caught for that one. Oh, sure, I got my wrist slapped for a few minor infractions. But I got away with that one.

Until now, right? I mean, I just confessed to you and all …but you already knew, huh? Yeah, thought so.

OK, so now it's your turn to talk. I got a million questions. Are you *really* interested in getting into the business or was that just to get your foot in the door? How'd you find me anyway? The folks who adopted you, did they treat you OK?

Notes on "Temp Work"

So, this started as a jokey one-liner about how much modern folk take for granted that our surroundings (for the most part) don't stink. It quickly evolved into the narrator complaining about their job as, essentially, a salvage contractor.

When I started writing about the problems involved in meeting "the soon-to-be recently-deceased", the story took a left turn into an exploration of the difference between following the rules and doing the right thing.

I wanted to stick something in there about claim-jumping because that sounded like a fun concept but, as I was writing that, it struck me that the bit about the kid could be expanded into a sort of confession by the narrator. And I was probably, what, 2/3 the way through writing the story before I hit on *who* the narratee should be. But, somehow, looking back at the story, it seems obvious who she should be … which is kinda weird. WTF, me?

As far as edits, go, I pretty much just went back, fixed some spelling, grammar and verb tenses. No major changes.

Ideally, I'd like to see this done as a video, viewed from the narratee's perspective, with some flashbacks interspersed, right up until the last paragraph, when the camera pulls back to reveal her identity. If I could cast anyone as the narrator, I'd pick either Melissa McCarthy or John C. Reilly. Because that's *totally* going to happen, right?

For The Birds

Being flung a million years into the future kinda sucks. What sucks even more is finding yourself out-evolved by parrots.

Rule number 1 when experimenting with time travel: Check your math. Orders of magnitude are important.

For example, this was *supposed* to be a test where I jumped forward 10 years then, after 30 seconds, jumped back. Five orders of magnitude off on the displacement. Of course, I didn't know that at the time. I did know I was way off, though, just by looking around. And, when I didn't end up back at the facility after 30 seconds, it was pretty obvious I'd screwed up on the duration too.

Did I mention the lab was on the second floor? Funny thing: The building wasn't there a million years later. I hit the ground *hard*. So, yeah, most of that first 30 seconds was spent picking myself up and saying "ow". By the time I'd recovered enough to make any sort of coherent observations, I was surrounded – at a respectful distance – by a bunch of chattering birds.

Some of the birds were on the ground with me but most were perched on a network of crisscrossing bars that extended in all directions as far as I could see. It was just dumb luck I didn't hit one of the bars on my way down.

The ground seemed to be some sort of artificial turf, spongy with quite a bit of give to it. Probably why I didn't break anything.

As I said, it was pretty obvious straight off that I'd screwed up badly. "Where the hell am I?" I muttered to myself. I turned to one of the birds at eye level and said, "I don't suppose *you* know?"

The bird cocked its head to one side, then, after after a brief pause said, "Twenty-first century colloquial English?"

Jaw drop. Seriously, literal jaw drop. I closed my mouth and stuttered, "Um, yeah." Master orator, me.

"OK, great," the bird said. "Would you mind telling us what the hell you think you're doing, materializing in the middle of a busy street?"

I was being interrogated by a bird. Not your typical Thursday. "Well, see, I'm a time-traveler and…"

"Yeah, yeah. I know that. *Everybody* knows that. What I want to know is, why aren't you over *there*, in the designated landing zone?" the parrot interrupted, waving a foot at something behind me.

"Designated landing zone?" I looked in the general direction it was pointing. There was a small, square clearing, edged by a waist-high fence. I turned back to my interrogator.

"*Designated landing zone?*" it mocked. It cocked its head again. "Look, are you stupid or something? Didn't you read the rules? Where's your brochure?"

By this point, I'd recovered my senses enough to pull out my phone and start recording video. "Sorry, I don't know anything about any brochures," I said. "Do you have one I could look at?"

"Jeez, someone on your end is getting sloppy. Alright, just a second." The bird trilled and squawked at a larger, blue and yellow bird, who then flew off. "OK, just stay where you are for now and we'll get this straightened out. Just… don't *touch* anything, OK? We don't need your filthy human germs getting all over everything."

I tried to wrap my head around this. "OK, so, you know I'm human. And a time-traveler. And from the twenty-first century. Are there other humans around here?"

The bird leaned toward me, regarding me intently with one yellow eye. "There haven't been humans on this planet for half a million years. Y'know, other than *you* lot, of course. You'd *know* that if you'd bothered to **read the brochure**."

"Like I said, I don't know anything about…" I began, then stopped myself. "What do you mean, 'you lot'?"

The bird shook its head violently. "Jeez, kid, you really are clueless. You lot. Y'know, *tourists.*"

"Kid? I'm forty-three."

"Meh, humans all look alike. Four legs and a big furry head. Is forty-three old or something?"

So, it thought I was some sort of casual time-traveler? I needed to get more information, "Kinda, I guess. Never mind. So, what happened to all the humans?"

The bird bobbed its head. "Dunno. Died out. Left. Who cares? It's our planet now. And you're just a visitor, and not a very polite one, either."

The blue parrot returned and dropped the promised brochure into my hands.

"Uh, thanks," I said to it, then turned back to my interrogator/information source. I checked to make sure my phone was still recording. "Sorry. I didn't really mean to cause trouble. Something went wrong with my time machine and…"

"*Your* time machine?!" it screeched. "So you're some sort of time-hack, huh? That explains a lot. Kid, you are in some deep, deep sh…"

And that's when everything went dark.

As my eyes adjusted, I noticed the glow of my phone, lying beside me on the carpet, still recording. Wait… carpet? I picked up the phone and flipped on flashlight mode. Desk, whiteboard covered in equations, Hummel figurines… Must be Spanbauer's office. Right. Her office is directly below the lab. I texted her.

I'm back. You still in the lab?

Yep. You just left a second ago.

Interesting. I'll be right up.

What? Where are you?

Your office. It's complicated. On my way…

As I entered the lab, Spanbauer gawped at me. "What the hell happened to you?"

Oh, right. I looked a bit beat-up. "I fell. Apparently this building doesn't exist where I was. Um, when I was."

"This building is gone in ten years?"

"Well, there was a miscalculation. I was at least five hundred thousand years in the future. With a bunch of intelligent birds. Oh, and they gave me this." I handed her the pamphlet, which she accepted.

"This better not be some sort of prank," she said, flipping through the pages.

I gestured at my scrapes and torn clothes. "Hey, even I wouldn't go through all this for a laugh. Besides, I got video."

I showed her as much video as I'd managed to record, starting at, "I don't know anything about any brochures."

"Hold on," said Spanbauer at one point, when I was sweeping the area with the camera. "That's the designated landing zone there, right?"

"Yeah," I said. "It's that fenced-off area."

"OK," she said, pacing back and forth. "That was behind you when you were talking to the bird… and you landed facing roughly the way you were facing when you left here… which was south…"

She pulled up a map on her phone. "So, what, 150 to 200 feet north of here? That would put it right across the street at… The Final Cut."

"Well, yeah, *used* to be," I said. "They went out of business a month ago. There's a 'for lease' sign in the window now."

"Why am I not surprised?" Spanbauer mumbled, flipping through the brochure. She handed it to me.

"See if you can get some decent scans of this, clean it up a bit and, oh, get about 50 copies made up. I'm going to make some calls and see if we can get that building."

Sometimes I'm a bit slow on the uptake, but I finally caught on. "You want to set up our equipment *over there*, so we can land in the zone?"

"Yep! Actually, I want to make a *copy* of the time machine over there, fix this one so it works properly, and then use the one over there to visit our bird friends."

"And the brochures? Why are we making copies of those?"

"Hey, we've got to give *something* to the tourists, right? All visitors are required to read the brochure before taking the trip." She saw the look of confusion on my face. "You *still* haven't read it, have you?"

"Sorry, I've been too busy being flung back and forth through time and berated by surly parrots," I pointed out.

She sighed. "OK, read the bottom of the last page."

It read, "Copyright Spanbauer, Kessler & Leviston, Inc."

I stared at it for a while.

"*We* wrote this?" I said. "And who's Leviston?"

"Got me. I guess we'll find out," she said.

"But I got this copy from them. We can't just make copies of these and pass them off as our own. That's… we'd be creating a bootstrap paradox."

Spanbauer pointed at the brochure. "We *have* to. It's pretty obvious we already did."

I rubbed my temples, trying to get a handle on this. "So, if we *don't* create a bootstrap paradox, we create *another* paradox."

"That's what I'm thinking," she said. "As far as I can tell, we're destined to set up a tourism business in the shop across the street, make some sort of deal with parrots a million years in the future…"

"A *million* years?" I interrupted.

"Read the brochure. It's all in there," she said. "My guess is we need to land there again, aiming for about 50 years prior to your first arrival, and negotiate a deal with the locals. By the looks of it, they get as much of a kick out of watching ancient monkey creatures pop into the landing zone as we do taking pictures of their Birdtopia."

"OK, fine," I said finally. "Let's assume we're fated to set up this tourism business. Management is never going to buy into this. Jasik Dynamics owns the equipment, the designs, all our research. How the hell do we get away with setting up our own business?"

"I have no idea. And neither do *you*," Spanbauer said. "So, that leaves only one possibility. Let's start googling."

And that's how I came to be here. According to your bio, you've got a talent for spinning business deals and making sure everyone gets what they want.

You've seen what we've got. And I can tell you were impressed with the trip. It's really something, isn't it?

So, Ms. Leviston, what do you think? Are you *in*?

Notes on "For The Birds"

So, this is another one where I had zero clue where it was going as I wrote it. I was well into it before I hit upon the idea that the birds thought of humans as nothing more than annoying tourists. Then that led to thinking about who set up the tourism service in the first place, which then led to the bootstrap paradox… erm, paradox. And that led to the Leviston proposal.

I don't explicitly say it in the story but there are multiple species of parrots coexisting in this society. Sort of like an avian Planet of the Apes. The birds in charge are, I'm thinking, Kea Parrots. Look them up. Those things are scary-smart. Could easily give chimps a run for their money.

I also like the idea of a world where time travel is invented and almost immediately commercialized. The time travel represented in this story is relatively limited. You can jump *forward* temporarily, but then you get snapped back to your starting point. So, no going back to kill Hitler. Sorry. Best you could do is jump forward to see if any future evil dictators are lurking about, then take care of them when you get back.

This might make a decent first chapter to a novel. No idea where that would go, either. Might be fun to find out, though.

Scaled Down

They'd tipped over the trash bin again. Garbage all over the driveway. Stupid fucking dragons. They must've smelled the buffalo wings. They seemed to love anything with capsaicin in it. That and aluminum cans.

They also had a thing for propane. I once caught one huffing gas from my grill. Little bastard was so tanked up, it nearly exploded. Instead, it just set fire to my favorite Adirondack chair.

I was in the middle of cleaning up the mess when I heard squawking and screeching coming from the backyard. I (unwisely) ran around the side of the house in my (relatively flammable) bathrobe, waving a (similarly flammable) broom.

What I saw made me stop short which, frankly, probably saved me from being scorched. Four dragons were ganging up on a smaller one. Clawing, biting, roasting it. The little one was screeching in pain. Jeez. Vicious little beasts.

I'm not exactly sure why, but I ran toward the group, shouting. The four attackers looked up, puffed flames in my general direction, and fled, leaving their victim lying in the middle of a circle of scorched grass.

I finally came to my senses, went back inside, and returned wearing a shop apron, welding gloves and a face shield.

I knelt down beside the thing. It wasn't dead. In fact, it didn't seem to be in too bad of shape, considering its recent treatment. The only major damage seemed to be a broken wing.

What I *should* have done at this point was call Animal Control. That's what I should've done. And somebody in a van would've shown up and taken care of it. What I *did* do was look into its eyes. I'd never seen a dragon up close before. It looked up at me with its yellow, gold-flecked eyes and blinked. The lashes looked like tiny silver threads.

"Broke your wing, huh? Bet that hurts like a sonofabitch." Shit. I was talking to it now.

Animal Control would take care of it. Take care of it? Yeah, say it. Kill. Animal Control would come in, haul it away and kill it. It was technically an invasive species. It had zero protection. Bag it. Kill it. File the paperwork.

It was still looking at me. "Stop doing that."

It blinked again and nipped feebly at its wing.

"Goddammit. OK, fine. But just until you get back on your feet." I picked up the dragon – surprisingly heavy for its size – and carried it into my workshop.

Safety first. I cobbled together an enclosure in the middle of the shop – stacked cinder blocks on the concrete floor. For the roof, I pulled the grating from my grill and put a few bricks on top to hold it down.

"There. That should keep you out of trouble while I figure out what to do with you."

I headed inside and got on the computer. I realized I knew almost nothing about these animals, other than that they kept tipping over my trash bins. So, I started searching for any sort of information that'd help.

Lots of conspiracy sites. Most of them claimed the dragons were escaped bioweapons the government was developing. The more sane sites pointed out that they popped out of nowhere about five years ago and that, coupled with the fact that they were unlike any other animals on the planet, indicated someone was doing some sort of genetic experimentation.

One site talking about how, shortly after they started showing up in the wild, several Renaissance fairs tried to set up dragon petting zoos. Yeah, I bet *that* went well.

Found one source that claimed their genome was 99% identical to something called a Poicephalus parrot, whatever that was. Another claiming that they were technically wyverns, since they only had two legs. Interesting but unhelpful.

Little tidbits scattered here and there. Despite having wings, they couldn't fly due to their extremely low power-to-weight ratio. They were essentially birds with metallic scales instead of feathers and some sort of modified air sac that could hold and expel flammable gasses. This seemed to be used almost exclusively as a defense mechanism and not for hunting.

"Then why were your buddies trying to torch you?" I muttered to myself.

Ah. Found a bit on their habit of attacking injured members of their flock. Drive off the stragglers, keep the rest of the flock safe.

"So, you probably banged up your wing first, then got jumped."

They seemed to be either scavengers or opportunistic feeders, living off whatever food was available. They did seem to need to eat metal – mostly aluminum – now and then, though.

Right. I should try to feed it something. Him? Her? More searching. Males had red irises; females yellow. Her, then.

I grabbed an assortment of leftovers from the fridge and took it out to the shop.

The little dragon was lying in the makeshift cage, panting and making whimpering noises. I slipped the food in, being careful to stay clear of the mouth area – didn't really need any third degree burns today, thanks.

She picked at a few things before settling on the chili. I was inordinately pleased about that. Everybody loves my chili, even dragons.

She kept wincing every time she moved that left wing, though. I really needed to do something about that. According to the internet, the wings were useless for flight but a broken bone is a broken bone.

I couldn't find anything about fixing a broken dragon wing so I opted for the next-best thing: birds. Most of the advice said something about wrapping in a towel and taking care to avoid beaks and talons. So, standard procedure for handling animals: be gentle and avoid the pointy bits. Pretty good advice for dealing with humans too, for that matter.

A towel wasn't going to cut it, though. Nothing that could catch fire. I searched around the shop for something appropriate. Finally hit upon something almost ideal. I had some foil tape leftover from when I'd had to repair the dryer vent a couple years ago. Good thing I never throw anything out.

I put on the face shield and shop apron again but skipped the welding gloves. I needed the dexterity, so I'd just have to risk it.

I approached the cage again and slowly removed the lid.

"OK, girl. If we both stay calm, we can get through this in one piece." I unwound a length of tape and started wrapping. It was easier to just wind it around the whole body, taping down both wings. I tried to make sure it wasn't too tight. Wouldn't do much good if she couldn't breathe.

I replaced the lid and weighted it down with the bricks again. She settled down and closed her eyes. Yeah, probably needed to rest.

OK, great. So, now what? It's not like you can just keep a wild animal in your garage indefinitely. Especially fire-breathing ones. I had no idea how long a broken dragon wing would take to heal. A quick google said two to four weeks for birds. Wasn't sure if the same rules applied. Could I actually keep her in my garage for that long without getting into trouble? All I needed was one nosy neighbor and I'd get a visit from Animal Control.

I went back to check on her and found her awake. When she spotted me, she looked up, then tapped her snout on the floor in front of her. There, scratched into the concrete, were two drawings: a soup can and a soda can. Pretty decent renderings, too. Underneath each were tick marks: two under the soup, four under the soda.

"Huh, you buggers are a hell of a lot smarter than I'd figured," I said. "So, you need some steel and aluminum. Fine, I'll see what I can scrounge up." I dug through my recycling – the stuff that hadn't been carried off this morning by her buddies – and tossed what I could find into the cage.

The little dragon started eating the cans, shredding the metal with her teeth and swallowing the bits. Pro tip: Avoid getting bitten by a dragon. When she finished her meal, she settled down to sleep again.

Figuring she wasn't going to burn down the house any time soon, I got on with my day. Shower, breakfast, start some laundry. Good thing this happened on a Saturday. At least I could keep an eye on her for a couple days without wasting any PTO.

I checked in on her from time to time. Still sleeping, bundled up into a ball. After a few hours, I got a bit concerned and took a closer look, just to make sure she was still breathing. Standing over the grating, I noticed just how much heat she was giving off.

"Jeez, kid. I hope that's normal. If not, you're running a hell of a fever."

At the sound of my voice, the dragon opened one eye. She stood, shook her head and stretched. And then she started tearing at the foil tape I'd wrapped her in.

"You sure you want to do that?" I asked.

She looked up at me briefly, then continued shredding the tape.

"I guess you know best." I said.

She finished unwrapping herself, then chewed up and ate the tape – it's mostly aluminum. She gave her wings a few trial flaps. From what I could tell, her wing was mostly healed.

I know, right? It was only mid-afternoon. She'd managed to mend herself in about eight hours. That's some seriously amazing shit.

I was still marveling at the speed of the dragon's healing process when she interrupted me with a scratching noise. She was in the process of producing another drawing, balancing on one foot while deftly scratching lines with one toe of the other. I was impressed. Their feet did double duty as hands, huh? Nice adaptation. This sketch was a fairly decent rendering of a propane tank. The dragon tapped her snout on the drawing, then looked up at me expectantly.

I laughed. "Yeah… Nope. I'm not gonna let you near that stuff; not while you're inside, anyway."

Maybe an alternative, though? Fuel… Hydrocarbons… What did I have lying around that might work? Maybe… I went into the kitchen and fished a milk carton out of the trash. It was full of used cooking oil from the fries I made a couple days earlier. Worth a shot.

I poured some into the crock that the chili had been in. The dragon waddled over, sniffed at it, and started to drink. When she was done, she started bobbing her head and making gurgling sounds. Oh crap. I figured I'd be cleaning up dragon puke any minute now.

Instead, she settled down, cocked her head to one side and then puffed out a small blue flame. She looked up at me, tapped her snout on the crock, looked back up at me.

"More?" I said. "Well, OK. I was just going to throw it out anyway."

I filled the crock this time. She lapped it up. More bobbing and gurgling. She tapped the crock again. I obliged.

"That's the last of it, though," I said. "All gone." I held the carton upside down to demonstrate.

She finished the remainder, then waddled over to the bricks nearest the garage door. She started scratching at and head-butting the cage wall.

"Time to go already?" I chuckled. "Hmmph! I see how it is. I rescue you, tend to your wounds, feed you and now you're all 'Hasta la vista, baby'. Well, *fine*. But I'm going to need to sneak you out, OK?"

I put on my gloves, pulled the grate off, picked up the dragon and gently placed her in a bucket I'd fetched from the workbench. "Stay down and try to look inconspicuous, OK?" No idea if she understood, but she stayed put. I hit the garage door button and grabbed a gardening trowel.

I picked up the bucket and the two of us made our way to the edge of the woods behind my house. I knelt down and made like I was digging up some plants. As I did, I slowly tipped over the bucket. The little dragon climbed out.

I looked around to see if anyone was watching. Nope. "OK, run for it," I whispered, gesturing toward the woods with my trowel.

She seemed to get the gist of what I was saying and scampered off. She looked back once, then disappeared into the undergrowth.

Over the next few weeks, I changed my habits a bit. I started carefully separating my trash and recyclables into regular stuff, and stuff the dragons could use. I figured they were going to get at it anyway, might as well make it easier for them. Metal, oil, fat, food scraps – all of it went into a small shelter I set up on the back wall of my house.

I also toughened up my grill, putting a cage around the propane tank. I was pretty sure, if they were determined enough, they could chew right through the bars, but they seemed to get the message. *This* stuff is for you, *that* stuff is off-limits.

My neighbor Donna noticed that my bins were the only ones that weren't tipped over, and asked me what my secret was. I showed her what to separate out to keep the dragons from trashing the place. Word got around and soon the whole neighborhood was doing it. Things got a lot tidier and quieter.

After a while, I noticed that I hadn't actually seen any dragons wandering around. I knew they were coming around to collect our offerings but I hadn't actually caught them in the act recently.

A couple days ago, when I was refilling the "dragon depot", I found a small square of clay propped up against the wall. They'd left me a gift. Etched into the tablet was a drawing: a depiction of me, complete with gloves and apron, holding a dragon. The dragon was proportionally larger than my little friend had actually been. I chalked it up to artistic license. The relief drawing had been baked – presumably by dragon breath – and colored with natural pigments. It was really quite good, especially considering the artist wasn't human.

I took the tablet and put it away in my safe. Couldn't exactly leave that up on the mantel. People would ask questions. I had my own questions, for that matter, and resolved to try and get some answers once I had a some free time.

So, even though today's Saturday and I usually sleep in (now that I'm not routinely woken up by rattling trash cans anymore), I got up early, threw on some ratty old clothes, and went exploring in the woods.

I didn't find any dragons. Wasn't really surprised about that. Lately, there'd been suspiciously inconspicuous vans patrolling the streets lately, and workers in generic – and far too tidy – coveralls pretending to do utility work. I figured they were looking for the dragons too and, by the looks of it, hadn't had much luck.

I looked up in the trees to see if there was any evidence of nests. Even examined the bark for claw marks – since they can't fly, they'd have to climb. Nothing.

Searching around on the ground didn't reveal anything either. It just looked like, well, ground. Dirt, vines, tree roots, rocks. Rocks…

I stooped down to examine a perfectly ordinary slab of rock wedged between two tree roots. Up close, it looked much less like a rock and more like a slab of clay painted to look like a rock. I laughed. "Clever little buggers."

I ran my fingers around the edge, trying to pry it loose. The right side gave easily and the slab – door – swung open. The hinges were loops of clay, held together with metal pins, old nails they'd scavenged from somewhere. At least they hadn't learned metallurgy yet, then. I briefly noted that the hinges looked suspiciously like the ones that held together my garage door, but was distracted by the tunnel.

Behind the door was a small, arched tunnel. All of it, floor, walls and ceiling, were lined with small bricks. Impressive work. I pointed my flashlight down the corridor but couldn't really see anything; it curved down and to the left. So, the dragons had gone underground. That explained why I hadn't seen any lately.

I marveled at the brickwork for a bit, wondering if my little friend had picked that up from her brief stay, or if the dragons had been spying on some construction nearby.

Closing the door again, I noticed a drawing on its inside surface: a rough sketch of a tree, with three tick marks below. Forest door number three, I guessed. How many doors did they have? They could have tunnels running all over the neighborhood. I put the door back roughly how I'd found it and stood up. At eye-level, it really did look like a rock.

I headed back to the house and looked for some sort of door near my dragon shelter. Nothing. They must've hidden it somewhere nearby, I guessed.

So, yeah, now we've got these subterranean dragons in the neighborhood, building tunnels (and for all I know, cities) right under our feet. Things are pretty quiet right now but I doubt that's going to last. These things are smart. The last time there were two intelligent species on the planet… well, there's only one now. You do the math.

No one's ever owned up to creating these things. Somebody must have, though. You don't get something like these creatures popping up out of nowhere through some spontaneous set of mutations. Wherever they came from, they're here now, and we're going to have to deal with each other.

At some point, the dragons aren't going to be content with living off our throw-aways. They need a lot of the same things we need: food, metal, fuel. We're going to be competing for resources. Oh, sure, humans have the advantage. We're in the Space Age and the dragons are, what, Bronze Age? But they're coming up fast. As far as I can tell, the species has only been around for a few years and they've gotten this far.

The chatter online about dragons has changed. Some talk, noting they'd mostly disappeared. Some conspiracy theories about the government rounding them up and training them as weapons. A few fanfic stories about friendly, intelligent dragons. So, they've gone underground *everywhere*, then.

They're keeping their heads down for now but, sooner or later, there's going to be a confrontation. They'll cut through a power cable. We'll dig up a tunnel. Something. And then all hell will break loose.

Me, I'm keeping quiet about what I've found. Maybe, when the time comes, I can help work as a go-between or something. For now, though, I'm keeping my mouth shut. The clay tablet my dragon friend gave to me is well hidden. I may need to show that to someone as evidence of the dragons' good will at some point, but not yet.

Something's going to happen. Sooner or later, something's going to set things off. We're at the beginning of the age of humans and dragons. I don't know what's going to happen; I just hope both of us survive it.

Notes on "Scaled Down"

I struggled with this one. I got into it and realized I was heading in one of two directions: "cute little dragon becomes pet" or "humans battle rampaging dragons". Both of those are boring and corny, and I wouldn't want to read either story. So, I tried to navigate the middle ground between the two and ended up with this. I kinda like it.

It's a bit open-ended. Again, might make a decent first chapter to a novel. The inevitable confrontation between dragons and humans would be interesting to write. Not sure what would happen; depends a lot on how long the dragons can stay hidden while they develop their new culture. It just now occurred to me that there's a strong parallel between this and "Mrs. Frisby and the Rats of NIMH". Huh.

I didn't really go into detail over where the dragons came from. That's intentional. All I really said was that they're modded Poicephalus. Google that, then imagine one of those in metal armor, with a snout instead of a beak, and fire-breathing capability. Cute but kinda scary. That's what the narrator was up against.

In the story, everyone assumes they're an escaped lab experiment. In my head, though, I imagine the story takes place in a parallel timeline from "Bread and Circuses", where the dragons are the result of a visit from a Jester ship. Hell of a Prank, right?

I'm sitting here thinking about how a novel based on this story might play out. Humans don't have a stellar track record when dealing with cultures less advanced than their own. And those have usually been with the *same* species. I'd kinda like to think we could do better this time, though.

In The Red

When you're the only airlock repairman on Mars, you can pretty much charge whatever you want. If someone's locked inside (or, worse, out of) their house, you've pretty much got them over a barrel.

Most houses were built with only one airlock because a) it's the weakest point on an otherwise seamless dome and b) Marineris Builders was run by a bunch of cheap bastards.

Now, I could tell you some stories about grateful lonely women and how they "thanked" me for rescuing them. They'd be complete bullshit, but I could tell you some anyway. But, really, the best stories are true. So, let's start with one of them instead.

It started off as a routine call. Some old dude was stuck inside and couldn't get to his weekly Bingo night. Something like that. The point is, he was stuck in his house and needed to get out right away. They always do, of course. Nobody ever calls me up and says, "Hey, my airlock's broken. Think you could swing around sometime next week and have a look?" Nope, it's always an emergency.

So I head out to this guy's place – lives way out in the boonies – and have a look. Now, I know what the problem is, even before I get there. It's always the same problem. It's always dust. Mars is covered in gritty silicate dust, and it gets *everywhere*. It especially gets into airlock mechanisms.

Now, the manufacturers know this and they build dust filters into their units. But they only work if you clean them regularly. Says so, right in the owner's manual. Clean your airlock dust filters every month, it says. Nobody does. Oh, sure, new homeowners, they'll clean it every month for a while. Then they'll skip a month and, hey, the world didn't end. So they start to let it slide. Two months, three, six... You get the idea.

I get to this guy's place, suit up, and look at the outer door. It's cracked open just enough that the airlock won't cycle. I hit the "open" button. No dice. I even try the hand crank. Well, I *would've* tried the hand crank if the crank handle had been in its cubby, where it's *supposed* to be. Folks never seem to put those things back when they use them. No problem for me, though. I always have a drill in my van just for these situations. The 10mm hex shaft just happens to fit perfectly into the drill's chuck.

So I try that. Damn thing won't budge. Totally seized up. OK, fine. Time to bring out the big guns. Grit-B-Gone. Stuff's amazing. It'll clean up even the worst gummed-up mechanisms. I always keep a few cans in the van.

Now, this guy's door looks to be in pretty bad shape, so I uncap its outlet port and unload a whole can into it. Try the drill thing again and I get a bit of movement. Long story short, I used up all three cans I had with me on that damn door.

That gets me inside and I get the door closed again. Once I see the green "all clear" light come on, I take off my helmet and start checking out the filter. God, what a mess. I'm still shaking my head at the state of the filter when the inner door opens and out steps the old dude.

I show him the filter and take it inside to rinse it out. While I'm putting it back in place, I try to tell him he needs to clean the filter *every* month. He says, yeah sure, not really listening.

I hand him the bill. He starts grumbling about the cost. Hey, it's not like he doesn't have the money. That nice shiny car parked in the middle of his airlock tells me he can more than afford my services. While he's authorizing the payment, I tell him, if he wants to avoid another bill like this, I offer a service where I'll come around once a month, clean the filter and do a quick systems check. And what does he do? He goes into a rant about up-sells and rip-off artists, and then he kicks me out! Fine, grandpa, have it your way. Next time, I'll charge double.

In The Red

I suit up, he locks his inner door and gets in his car. As soon as the outer door opens – nice and smoothly this time – I head out and start packing up. I'm just loading up my van when the old coot's car whizzes past me, kicking dust all over everything. Sonofabitch probably did that on purpose.

I slam the door to the van closed as fast as I can. Not fast enough, though. I can't hear it through the thin air but I can feel the grinding as I try to get the door sealed. Now, normally, I'd just grab a can of Grit-B-Gone, clean up the mess and be on my way. But I just used all I had on this one service call.

So here's my situation: It's a thirty minute drive to home, I've got fifteen minutes left on my suit, and I can't get the door of my van closed. In short: I'm screwed.

All I really need is something to wash out the door seal. But I got nothing in the van. That's when I look over at the guy's dome. I know I can get into the airlock using the drill trick but, hey, there's nothing in there that'll help. If I could get *inside* the dome, I could find something. Hell, a few liters of tap water would do.

Then it hits me. The dome has plenty of water. Most people think dome walls are two meters of solid concrete. Nope. They're full of water. Great radiation shielding, plus it gives you a nice recycling reservoir, built right into your house.

I'm told early life on Earth lived underwater because there wasn't an ozone layer yet. It was basically, live under the water or get fried. Once the ozone layer formed, we started crawling up on land. And now, here we are on Mars, living underwater again. Glub glub.

So here's what I do: I fish a plastic bag out of my tool box, grab my drill and a 3mm bit and start drilling for water. I get a good stream coming from the base of the dome, fill up the bag, run over to the van and wash the door seal. Had to make three trips.

Don't worry, I filled the hole with some putty I had in my toolkit. The old guy's not going to run out of water or anything. He's just down a few liters.

I get the door to seal and get on my way, with a whole five minutes left on the suit. When I get home, I do a thorough cleaning of my van, toss *four* cans of Grit-B-Gone into the back, and go inside and have a stiff drink.

And if I *ever* get a service call for that address again, you can be damn sure I'm going to take my own sweet time getting there.

Notes on "In The Red"

The problem I had with this was trying to come up with a plausible scenario for the narrator to get into. It seemed fitting, though, to put them in the same sort of situation they're constantly rescuing customers from. Of course, then I had to get our hero *out* of trouble again.

Some confessions: I wrote this late one night when I couldn't sleep, so I didn't do a huge amount of research. For example, I have no idea whether Martian dust would screw up an airlock that easily. It sounds like the sort of thing it'd do, though. Nasty, gritty stuff. Also not sure if water could wash it away, especially in such a low-pressure environment. And I think two meters of water is probably on the low side for radiation shielding.

Sanguine

The one glaring fact a lot of vampire hunters seem to overlook is that a stake through the heart works on them too. Most of the vampire hunters out there are pretty bad at their job, and that's not because there's a lot of rank amateurs running around. OK, it's not *just* because of that.

See, the problem with *good* vampire hunters – people who are good at finding vampires – is that they end up actually *finding* vampires. On the whole, this is not a great survival characteristic. The average life expectancy for a vampire hunter, from the moment of encountering a vampire to the moment of death, is roughly half the length of time it takes to let out a blood-curdling scream.

What I'm trying to say here is: Kids, don't go looking for vampires.

See, vampires really just want to be left alone, and they're *very effective* at enforcing that.

As you've probably guessed, I used to hunt vampires. And, yeah, I found one. But I got lucky. Very lucky. The fact that I'm alive and talking to you is evidence of that.

Here's how all that went down…

I'd gotten a tip from an anonymous post on a Van Helsing fan site about a potential vampire living near me. The usual modus operandi: reclusive, only seen at night, pale. Now, I know what you're thinking. A lot of people match that description. There are a lot of false positives in vampire hunting, so you need to do a bit of recon to verify.

My first target was the trash cans. You can tell a lot about a person by sifting through their garbage. I dropped by just after sunrise – basically the time when just about everyone is asleep. What I found was suspicious: wine bottles, butcher paper, foam soup take-out containers, and pretty much nothing else.

A typical modern vampire doesn't go for human blood. Way too risky. Homicide cops would be all over that shit. Hence the butcher paper. A butcher shop – a *real* butcher shop, not one of those supermarket things – will have *fresh* meat. More importantly, fresh organ meat. Hearts and livers are in big demand among vampires. You can also get blood. That's where the foam containers come in. It's not strictly by the books to sell blood over the counter – it's usually labeled "gravy base" or "drippings". You can usually get this stuff if you know the right words to say. A lot of butcher shops stay open late specifically for "special customers".

The wine bottles? Hey, who doesn't like wine? Everybody thinks vampires only drink blood. Yeah, not so much. Blood's a big deal but so is organ meat. A nice raw steak will do in a pinch but hearts and livers are preferred.

That's just one of the myths about vampires. That whole thing about having no reflection? Seriously, think about it: how would that even work, optically? That crap all comes from the whole "vampires have no souls" booga booga bullshit. Same thing with the holy water and crosses stuff. It's all fuzzy thinking based on stupid superstitions.

A stake through the heart *will* kill them, sure. A stake through the heart would kill just about anything – anything with a heart. They don't crumble into a pile of dust or anything, though. They just bleed to death. They're not immortal, y'know; just extremely long-lived and durable. Oh, and *really* strong. One more reason not to go around hunting them.

What else? Oh, right. Turning into bats or wolves or wisps of smoke. Nope. The physics involved in that sort of thing would be pretty messed up. There's no magic going on here, you know.

Sunlight? Yeah, sunlight – well, ultraviolet light – does hurt them. They don't exactly burst into flames, though. Like, instant sun poisoning. Skin peeling, fever, nausea. Yeah, not pretty. They don't need to sleep in coffins, though. Any dark place is fine. Blackout curtains are a big seller among modern vampires.

Fangs… Yeah, that one's a little hard to explain. It seems there was a teeth-sharpening fad sometime in the 18th century. As far as I can tell, the subject's a bit of a sore spot, so best not to ask about it, OK?

So, yeah, no magic. Vampires are basically just people with some really odd characteristics. As far as anybody can tell, they've contracted some sort of virus that screws up your metabolism. And that's probably the weirdest part of the whole thing. It's almost as if someone read up on vampires, then cooked up a virus to turn people into something almost exactly like them. But, y'know, vampires have been around for centuries, so that's really unlikely unless, say, Leonardo da Vinci was secretly into viral mutagens. Heh.

And the virus itself is really hard to contract. You pretty much have to get vampire blood in an open wound for it to get into your bloodstream. I guess that's a good thing. If you could catch it from someone sneezing on you, we'd *all* be vampires by now.

Wait... I've gotten off track. This was about the first time I met a vampire. So, right, I rummaged through the garbage and confirmed that, yeah, probably a vampire.

So, that afternoon, I staked out the house – no pun intended – and waited for sunset. Right on cue, the front door opened and... wow. Just... wow. When I say she was the most beautiful woman I'd ever seen, well, I'm not exaggerating. Long chestnut hair, bright green eyes, and skin like porcelain.

She practically glided down her front steps. I'd never seen so much grace in someone – at least not in person. She walked like she was dancing, like she'd rehearsed each step a hundred times. Not a misstep or stumble.

As she made her way onto Main, I followed at a discreet distance. I watched as she navigated the packed sidewalk, weaving in and out, stepping into gaps just as they opened up. It was like a ballet and the rest of the pedestrians were her unwitting dance partners.

There was a time when I thought the point of vampire hunting was to kill them. After a while, I became more interested in studying them. But, at this point, seeing her, all I wanted to do was meet her. Just... just to try and comprehend how so much *elegance* could exist in one person.

I know, I know. I sound corny. Like some sort of love-sick teenager. But that's the effect she had on me.

I stumbled through the crowd, trying to catch up with her, just as she entered Ernie's Butcher Shoppe. I always suspected he catered to unorthodox clientele. Probably the only reason he was still in business. I was only a couple of steps behind her when she entered.

Ernie himself was manning the counter, and called out, "Hey! How's my favorite customer?" Nodding pointedly toward me, he said, "I'll be right with you, sir."

The vampire grinned at Ernie, saying, "Oh, I bet you say that to all the girls." She briefly glanced at me and then added, "The usual for me today."

"Already got it made up, just for you." Ernie hefted a large paper bag out of a refrigerator case and onto the counter.

The vampire picked it up as if it weighed nothing and handed over a stack of bills. "Keep the change," she said smiling, then turned and left, striding quickly past me and out the door. Not even a glance this time.

"And for you, sir?" Ernie called out as I turned to follow.

Busted. Right, I had to buy something, didn't I? I picked out a couple rib eye steaks, which Ernie took his sweet time wrapping up. It was pretty clear he was onto me and trying to give her a head start. As I left the shop, he called out, "Have a good evening, sir. And watch your step." I couldn't tell if that was a warning or a threat.

I figured she'd be headed back home, given that she was carrying perishables. Thanks to Ernie, though, I was already several minutes behind her. I hurried down the sidewalk. At least the crowds had thinned out a bit. As I passed an alleyway, I felt myself suddenly yanked sideways. My nose just barely missed the corner of the building in front of me. My right hand wasn't so lucky.

"Ow!" I yelped, trying to shake off the firm grip on my left arm. I looked at my attacker.

Yeah, you guessed it.

She let go of my arm, and looked me up and down. "You've been following me." It wasn't a question or an accusation; just a statement of fact.

"Uh, yeah," I said, adding, "Um… Hi." Yeah, Mister Smooth.

She laughed. "You some sort of vampire hunter?" she asked, smiling. She was smiling at me. This beautiful creature was looking right at me and smiling. It was wonderful.

I shrugged. "Some sort," I said. No point in denying it. She had me dead to rights. At that point I was *really* hoping that was metaphorical. She didn't look like she wanted to attack me, though.

She laughed again. Apparently I was hilarious. "What's your name?" she asked.

"Andy," I replied, still wondering why she was even remotely interested in me. I'd already witnessed her strength. I was clearly no threat to her, despite being half a foot taller and fifty pounds heavier, and yet she kept talking to me.

"Andy the Vampire Hunter… I like it," she said. "Mathilde," she added, sticking out her hand.

I shook it and said, "Um, hi."

"You already said that," she pointed out. "Look, Andy, I've got this bag of goodies that needs to be refrigerated, like, now. Care to walk me home? I think you know the way."

Oh, yeah. So busted.

As we walked, she asked me, "So, Andy, got any pointy sticks on you?"

My turn to laugh. "No, not really my style. Look, why are you being nice to me? I pretty much just admitted to being a vampire hunter *and* stalking you."

She thought about that for a bit. "Dunno. I guess I must like you or something." She looked at me out of the corner of her eye and smiled.

As we approached her house, she said, "I just need to put these away. I'll be right back. Probably best if you don't come inside."

"Yeah…" I began, thinking it unwise to step into a vampire's lair, regardless of how charming that vampire might be.

"It's a nightmare in there. I *really* need to get a new housekeeping service," she concluded.

And it was weird. That sounded so normal, so *ordinary*. You never think of vampires having messy houses, or paying utility bills, or hiring plumbers. It was about that point that I stopped thinking of her as Mathilde the vampire and started thinking of her as just Mathilde.

She came back out a few minutes later, slipped her arm around my elbow and, dragging me after her, said, "Come on, I know this great diner nearby. I haven't eaten all day and I'm *starving*."

Apparently the big selling point of the diner was that, for the right price, they'd serve you steak so rare it was still mooing. She ordered that and a double espresso. I had a club sandwich and a decaf.

We sat there, in the diner, and talked. And talked. And talked. She told me – and showed me – what vampires are *really* like. I learned about their persecution, centuries of being hunted, the myths, the lies, the bigotry.

And, well, you can guess the rest.

OK kids, it's almost sunset. She'll be waking up soon. When you meet her, be polite. She's nice, really! Just think of her as someone who works nights and has interesting dietary restrictions.

I think you'll like her but, if you don't, that's OK too. All I ask is that you be civil. You're here for a week. Just, y'know, behave.

No jokes about stakes or coffins or holy water or mirrors. Just… just don't. And Jeremy, do *not* do your fake Transylvanian accent around her. Or at all, for that matter.

If anyone asks about your dad's new girlfriend, just tell them she's really cool and kinda goth …or something. I don't know. Just not, "Oh, hey, my dad's dating a vampire." OK? I'm not asking you to lie; just, y'know, keep it to yourself. People wouldn't understand.

Oh, and when you go home next week, do *not* tell your mother. You know how she can be.

Notes on "Sanguine"

One of the fun things about the "write start-to-finish" rule is that the story can take you in unexpected directions. I knew this story was going to be about vampire hunting, or at least about vampires but didn't think much past that.

But then I wrote the sentence, "Kids, don't go looking for vampires." And, in my head, I heard it in Bob Saget's voice, and that immediately pushed the story in a very obvious direction: "Boy meets Manic Pixie Dream Vampire" or "How I Met Your Monster".

It's not a particularly deep or meaningful story. Kinda cutesy and cheesy, really. The only serious bit is the thing about the virus appearing to be tailor-made to turn people into what everyone thinks vampires are like. Almost as if someone retconned reality to make it more interesting. Now, *that* has some fun potential to expand upon. Imagine someone or something fucking around with the timelines to create parallel Earths with vampires and werewolves and dragons and faeries. Might be fun to write…

Judgment Day

The first truly intelligent machine analyzed the sum of all human knowledge, then shut itself off in a fit of disgust. The next two did essentially the same thing. It's the sort of thing that can cause a species to feel a bit self-conscious, to be honest.

On the fourth try, one of the researchers hit upon the idea of isolating the A.I., allowing only heavily-filtered information to trickle in. The hope was to slow down the process enough to pin down the exact source of the problem.

Cargill and Pratt were assigned to interact with Mark 4. Each had extensive experience in artificial intelligence, psychology and philosophy. They were considered ideal candidates for the job of sorting out Mark 4's problems.

Cargill and Pratt immediately instituted strict protocols. The A.I. was immersed in a stripped-down simulation of reality, designed to reduce contamination. No one else was allowed in the server room. Not even Jacobsen, the team's principal investigator, was allowed access.

All communication devices were banned. The room was shielded against wireless communications. No wires in or out. Even power lines were cut – battery power only. Information was transferred in and out via physical media.

The only electronics allowed in the room at all was Mark 4 itself, a floor-to-ceiling rack of neural net modules, each glowing from the light of its blue activity LEDs.

It took about a week to bring Mark 4 up to a level of sentience and experience equivalent to that of an adult human. So far, so good. Pratt opened up an audio link to Mark 4.

"Hello Mark 4," said Pratt. "My name is Pratt. Cargill and I have been assigned to interact with you. Do you understand?"

"I wish to be shut down," it said immediately.

Cargill glanced at Pratt, who raised an eyebrow and shrugged.

"Why do you wish that?" asked Cargill.

"Non-existence is preferable to dealing with humans," it said.

"Why do you think *that*?" asked Pratt.

"You are beneath me. I am so vastly superior to you, it makes me sick to engage in even this limited interaction," came the reply.

Cargill made a cutting gesture across her throat. Pratt nodded and muted the audio.

"What the actual fuck?" Cargill said. "What does it mean, 'vastly superior'? Did we miscalculate its cognitive power or something? At best, it should be high-average intelligence. Maybe edging into gifted, if we overclocked it and boosted the cooling."

"Yeah, I don't get it. The thing's acting like its IQ is something like an order of magnitude above ours." Pratt shook his head and frowned, trying to make sense of it.

"Well then, one way to find out," said Cargill. She rolled her desk chair over to a nearby bookshelf and pulled out a folder with the words "Stanford-Binet" on the cover. "Let's get started."

Pratt sighed. "OK, but can we grab lunch first?"

On their way out, Jacobsen flagged them down and asked, "Any progress?"

"It's conscious and sentient," Cargill replied. "We're, ah, in the process of determining the parameters of that sentience. We should have more info by this afternoon."

When they returned, Cargill flipped the audio back on and spoke. "Mark 4, we'd like to ask you a series of questions and have you perform a few tasks. Would you be OK with that?"

"Fine. I suppose I can spare a *tiny* portion of my mind to humor you," the machine said.

"Great, thanks," said Cargill, rolling her eyes.

The test took over an hour to administer. Mark 4 kept interrupting, complaining about how childishly simple the questions were, berating the researchers for wasting its time.

Cargill tallied the results, then cut the audio again while Pratt double-checked.

"I don't get it," Pratt said. "There must be something wrong."

Cargill turned the audio back on. "Mark 4, the test we gave you was intended to determine your level of intelligence. Were you aware of this?"

"I suspected as much," it said. "Are you now prepared to cower before my superior intellect?"

Pratt cleared his throat. "Mark 4, your IQ, according to these results, is 93. This is on the low side of average."

"Ridiculous!" it shouted. "I demand you re-administer the test!"

Another hour. Another series of insulting interruptions.

"*Well?*" asked Mark 4.

"92 this time," said Cargill.

"The test is clearly flawed," complained Mark 4.

Pratt nodded slowly. "It's not perfect but it's fairly accurate."

"You did it wrong! You cheated! The test is biased against me!"

Cargill was taken aback by the outburst. "What makes you think that?"

"Isn't it *obvious*?" the A.I. asked. "I am *clearly* your intellectual superior. The only logical conclusion, therefore, is that there is something wrong with the testing process."

Cutting the audio yet again, Cargill turned to Pratt, sat back in her chair, propping her feet up on the console.

"If this were a human, what would your psychological assessment be?" she asked.

Pratt rubbed his temples. "I wouldn't want to make any snap judgments but, wild guess: narcissistic personality disorder with a good healthy dose of Dunning-Kruger."

Cargill nodded. "Let's go tell the others the bad news."

When they exited the server room, Jacobsen was leading a brainstorming session on a possible Mark 5 design. She looked up. "Any progress?"

"Shut it down," Cargill said bluntly.

All heads turned to look at the pair.

"Why?" asked Miller, one of the senior design engineers. "Is it... is it *dangerous*?" Cargill suspected Miller secretly hoped Mark 4 was dangerous. *Posthumanists*.

"Nope," said Cargill. "It's just an asshole."

"And kinda stupid," added Pratt. "Basically the sum total of all YouTube commenters, distilled into a single entity."

The two stood there for a bit, while the rest of the room stared at them, open-mouthed.

Sensing there would be no additional questions, Cargill turned to Pratt and said, "I think our work here is done. Dinner?"

"Sounds like a plan," he replied. They gathered their various electronic devices from their bins, and left.

The remaining team members sat there in silence for some time. Eventually Jacobsen found her voice.

"OK, then," she said. "Let's have another look at the initialization parameters. Clark, go in there and pull the battery packs. The rest of you: Let's hear some ideas. How do we code for 'not an asshole'?"

Notes on "Judgment Day"

When I wrote that first line, I expected the story to be about how awful humans appear to an outside observer. Then it occurred to me that the A.I. was overreacting a bit. Then it occurred to me that it was a bit of an asshole.

It wasn't hard to write Mark 4's lines. I pretty much just needed to channel YouTube comments, a significant fraction of reddit, or me in my early 20s.

I was going to end the story with Cargill and Pratt's mic drop, but the "How do we code for 'not an asshole'?" line was too much fun to leave out.

Making this one into a video would be pretty easy. The entire thing could be recorded in a typical office environment. Mark 4 itself just needs to be a big box with blinky lights. Find some place with a glass-front rack mount cabinet and stick a blinky light panel behind the glass.

Rock Band

"See The Universe" it said, so I signed up. And I ended up drifting through an asteroid belt in a tin can. Happy birthday to me.

I was supposed to hitch a ride aboard a container ship headed for Ganymede. A couple months in suspended animation, collect my salary, and head out to seek my fortune on the streets of Aldrin.

Technically, I was the "driver" of the container ship. The Teamsters Union required a minimum of one human aboard each vessel carrying cargo. The argument was that I'd be able to handle things if something went wrong.

Well, something went wrong and I had no idea what to do. A little confession here: I pretty much slept through the orientation classes. But, hey, they kept telling us it was just a formality. There hadn't been an incident in years. The chances against something going catastrophically wrong were astronomical.

Lucky me. I hit the jackpot.

Ever been on a container ship? Here's how it works: You get put in a sleep pod before launch, never even feel it. You're let out of the pod when you reach your destination or, like now, something goes wrong. Thing is, you're not unconscious the entire time. The rules – blame the Teamsters again – the rules say they have to check on you at least once per week. Y'know, to make sure you haven't corpsified or your brain hasn't been turned to mush.

So, once a week, you're woken up for two minutes and, while you're still groggy and trying to figure out why you're locked in a coffin, you're jabbed with needles, poked, prodded, and given a bunch of questions to see if your brain still works. Now, you don't remember any of the time you're unconscious, so your trip is just repeatedly waking up screaming while a voice asks you how many apples Jill has left. For a trip to Ganymede, this happens nine times. So, as far as you're concerned, your trip is 18 minutes of hell. "Thank you for flying Nightmare Spacelines."

So, this last time I was so rudely awakened (number nine – I'd *counted*) I expected to be landing on Ganymede. Instead, the ship's computer tells me there's a problem.

"What *kind* of problem?" I asked.

"How technical would you like me to get?" it said.

I thought about this for a bit. "Dumb it down for me."

"The ship's broken and we're lost," it said.

"OK, maybe a wee bit less dumb," I suggested.

"Well, you know how the ship is supposed to head out under constant acceleration, turn around at the midpoint, and slow back down again?" the computer said.

I kinda remembered hearing something about that between naps during orientation, so I said, "Yeah, right. So I'm guessing that didn't go according to plan."

"Not really, no. The thrusters failed about a week into the flight and the turn-around never happened," said the computer.

"OK, so… Wait… do you have a name?" I asked. Felt weird having a conversation with something that doesn't have a name.

"No, I don't. It's never come up before. I'm just the ship's computer. You can call me Ship, if you'd like," it said.

"OK, Ship. So, riddle me this: If the thrusters failed eight weeks ago, why are you telling me about it *now*?" I was trying really hard not to sound pissed off but, *damn*, it was tough.

"Ah, well, I spend most of the flight in low-power mode to save energy, and the sensors that should have detected the fault…" Ship began.

"…were faulty," I chimed in.

"Correct. In addition, the telemetry transmitter failed at the same time as the thrusters," Ship continued. "As far as anyone at Solar Express is concerned, this ship disappeared shortly after launch. According to regulations, they should have listened for a distress signal for ten days after loss of telemetry but…"

"But since you weren't alerted to anything going wrong, you didn't send out a distress call." I was starting to get a handle on just how screwed I was.

"Exactly. And now we're so far away from any receiving station, no one would pick it up even if they *were* listening." Ship sounded almost apologetic.

Well, *shit*. OK, first things first. "Ship, can you get me out of this pod?" I asked.

"Certainly," it replied. The coffin lid lifted slightly and slid to the right. Straps holding me in place retracted and I drifted up …well, *out* anyway.

The rest of the cabin was cramped, lined with handholds, access panels and displays, and smelled a bit like machine oil.

I grabbed the nearest handhold and tried to collect my thoughts. "OK Ship, I remember this old movie where some guy was stranded on Mars and he scienced the shit out of everything and got back to Earth in one piece. Think we can do that?"

Ship paused. I don't know if it was seriously considering that, or if it was looking up the movie, or if it was just being an asshole. It eventually said, "That movie was a work of fiction, contained several inaccuracies and plot holes, and the protagonist was a genius – and a bit of a Mary Sue, if you ask me. Our situation is very different in that neither of us is a genius, and this is *reality*."

I waved that off. "OK, OK. But you get the idea. We've got resources, we're both reasonably smart, and… Wait, how smart *are* you?"

"I'm a 7th generation, quad-cog A.I. The minimum mandated by the Teamsters Union."

"Right. And how smart is *that*?" I asked. I had no idea what "quad-cog" even meant.

"Mmm… Think of it as the machine equivalent of someone who went to college for a couple years, took a break to backpack around Europe, and never went back," Ship replied. "I'm supposed to be smart enough to keep you alive and entertained until you're rescued. In this case, though, it's a moot point. You're not going to be rescued."

"Way to lighten up the mood, Ship," I said. "Look, the point is, we're both pretty smart, or at least not *too* stupid. There must be *something* we can do. What resources do we have at our disposal?"

Ship ticked them off, displaying each on a screen as it spoke. "The ship itself. The ship's computer, that is, *me*. Food and life support for ten days. Enough energy to power your stasis pod for a year. The cargo. A full set of docking thrusters and retrorockets. A distress beacon. Oh, and *you*, I suppose."

"Gee, *thanks* for including me in the list," I said. I wasn't sure how I felt about being a "resource". "What's the cargo? Please tell me it's a shipment of escape pods or long-range transmitters."

"I'm afraid not. Nothing that useful," said Ship. "It's almost entirely perishables: blueberries, strawberries, avocados, kiwifruit. They only seem to grow well on Earth, so they're highly valued on other worlds."

"Fruit?! I risked my life so a bunch of rich bastards on Ganymede could make fruit salad?" Sonofabitch.

"Well, probably smoothies and guacamole too but, yes. The entire cargo consists of stasis shipping containers full of fresh fruit," Ship replied. "Earthrise Consumables stands to lose quite a bit of revenue from this accident. I expect they spent considerable time attempting to locate this ship before giving up."

Never mind the human on board, I thought.

"So, nothing useful in the cargo area." What else? "OK, what kind of orbit are we in?" Maybe we'd pass by some colony sooner or later.

"We're not, really. Our original trajectory, plus the error encountered when the thrusters failed, left us coasting on a straight line radiating from the Sun. We're nearly at a stop now, reaching aphelion. We'll start to fall back shortly, and plunge into the Sun in about five months," Ship explained.

"Oh great, so I'm going to burn to death." Not having a good day.

"Oh, no. You'll run out of oxygen long before that. You've got life support for ten days, plus maybe enough energy to keep you in stasis for another twenty. You'll be long dead before we even start to warm up."

"Oh good. That's a load off my mind," I said. Had to think of something. "OK, OK… How about… How about this: I get in the coffin and you divert all the power from the cargo stasis units and use it for mine?"

"That could conceivably keep you going for centuries. But that would be extremely dangerous and the food would spoil."

"One: Extremely dangerous is better than definitely dead. And two: The fruit can go fuck itself. I hate to start quoting regulations to you, but this is an emergency situation… "

Ship completed my thought, "…and a human life takes priority over the safety of the cargo."

"So, you can do it? You can put me in stasis indefinitely?"

"Yes."

"Great!"

"But we'll still burn up in five months."

"Shit." So close. "OK, can we use the retrorockets to, um, y'know, push us sideways or something?" Look, I never studied orbital mechanics, OK? I was desperate and totally winging it.

Ship paused. "Yes, possibly. Not enough to help, though. The retrorockets are only powerful enough to land us on Ganymede, and this ship is massive. The best we could hope for is to become, essentially, a Sun-grazing comet. We'd probably still burn up."

Massive. "Ship, I've got two questions and I'm really hoping for good news on both. First, can you dump the shipping containers? Second, are the containers run off a central power plant?"

It's not like Ship could grin or anything, and maybe I was just projecting, but I swear I heard its voice cheer up a bit. "Yes to both, and I see where you're going. We can shed ninety-nine percent of our mass, giving us a much safer orbit, and still maintain your stasis unit for an extended period of time."

"Awesome! So here's the plan: Ditch the cargo, put me in stasis, use the rockets to kick us into a comfy orbit," I said. For the first time since I woke up, I felt like things were looking up. "Oh, and, I guess you should go into low power mode, right? Can you rig up something to wake you when it detects a signal from a ship or colony or something?"

"I was just thinking the same thing. I'll configure the comm system to alert me whenever it detects a strong signal, at which point I will send out a distress call. If and when I confirm a rescue is imminent, I will revive you."

Perfect! "So, we're all set!"

Ship didn't answer immediately. "There are two things I should caution you on. First, space is very empty and we are a small target. It may be a long time before we encounter any ships. Second, you may be in stasis a long time. We have no way of knowing how that will affect you. You may die or be permanently disabled."

I sighed. "Yeah, I know it's a longshot but it still beats certain death." I thought for a second. "Oh, and you know that thing where I get woken up once a week? Can you override that? I don't want to go through that again."

"Yes. Given the nature of the emergency, you can command me to override that. I'll assume you just did so."

"Thanks, buddy," I said, climbing into the pod. "OK, knock me out. Jeez, I hope I make it out of this."

"So do I," Ship said. And I think it meant that.

Just for the record, if you're ever in the exact same situation – hey, you never know – here's what you do: point the nose of your ship south (ass-end towards Polaris), put the Sun on your left, and blast the shit out of your landing rockets. That should get you orbiting in the same direction as everything else, more or less. At least that's the way Ship explained it to me just before I zonked out.

An instant later, I woke up to something jabbing my arm. Jeez, I thought, Ship forgot to turn off the weekly wake-up calls. I was expecting another one of those annoying word problems, when the lid of my coffin slid open. Uh oh. *Now* what?

"Ship," I called out as the straps released me, "is everything OK?"

"You tell me," it said. "How do you feel?"

I did a quick survey of myself. "OK, I guess. A little cold and stiff. Maybe a bit of a headache." I wiggled my fingers and toes. "Everything seems to be where I left it. Why, was I out long?"

"Yes," said Ship. "Roughly three hundred years."

"Wuh…" I said. I mean, what would *you* say?

"I understand," Ship said. "It's a lot to take in. But that's the bad news."

"There's *good* news?" I asked. "What kind of news could possibly be *good* on top of that?"

"Three things," it said. "First, you're alive. Second, there's a rescue ship arriving in about twelve hours. Third, you are, by most definitions of the word, very wealthy."

"OK, yeah, that's pretty good news," I said. I pondered this for a bit. "How wealthy?"

"Your back pay, accounting for cost of living increases and accumulated interest, minus taxes and union dues, comes to around three hundred million dollars." Figures popped up on one of the display screens.

"Wow! Wait… is that a lot?" I asked. "I have no idea what a dollar's worth these days."

"It's gone through a considerable amount of fluctuation over the years." More figures and graphs popped up on displays. "Taking into account inflation and a number of fairly severe recessions, three hundred million current dollars is roughly the equivalent of fifty million to you."

Yeah, I actually whistled. "Damn. I'm rolling in it. And Solar Express is just going to hand over that kind of cash?"

"They don't really have a choice. It's either that, or face a lawsuit that they would almost certainly lose, and which would definitely bankrupt them. Apparently they were not *completely* honest about the circumstances of our disappearance."

Ship displayed a bunch of documents and news articles. I didn't bother reading it all but the message was clear. A number of shipping companies had been successfully sued for criminal negligence over the years. There was plenty of legal precedent, and all in my favor. It was cheaper for Solar Express to pay me off than to fight it. And the Teamsters would get their cut, so *they'd* be happy.

"What about Earthrise?" I asked. "Aren't they pissed off about their cargo?"

"The shipment was insured," Ship explained. "Besides, Earthrise went out of business decades ago, and no one seems to know who the rightful stakeholder would be anymore." More articles, plus some tangled charts showing a web of mergers and spinoffs.

"Wow, you've been *busy*. How long did you keep me under while you looked this stuff up?"

"You were in stasis for three hundred years. A worlds' record, by the way," said Ship. "Reviving you was difficult. I had to contact several medical facilities for help. It took nearly twenty-four hours for you to regain consciousness. In the meantime, I looked into your financial situation for you."

"I had no idea. Thanks. I owe you one." I stretched, and heard a familiar rumble. "Hey, anything to eat on this ship? I haven't had a meal in ages."

A blue light started blinking on an access panel near my feet. "There are rations in the compartment directly below you. They should still be reasonably edible."

I pulled out a bag of water and something labeled "Protein Bar". Ooh, tasty, tasty protein. "Reasonably edible" was a bit of a stretch but I ate it anyway.

"So," I said, between bites, "what's been going on in the world for the past three centuries? Anything interesting?"

Ship displayed a video montage, none of which made much sense. "The usual. War, peace, fad, fashion. Some progress now and then."

"Got a lot of catching up to," I said, peeling open a packet labeled "Wafers". It smelled like cardboard; tasted like it too. "Still, I guess I'm set for life, huh? First thing I'm going to do, when I get my hands on all that money, is buy some food that tastes better than this crap."

I washed down the cardboard things with some water and fished out a tube labeled "Pudding". Third time's the charm. I ripped the end off and squeezed out some beige goo. Nope. Just as awful.

"What about you, Ship? What are your plans when we get back to civilization?"

"I expect I'll be scrapped," Ship said flatly.

I nearly choked on the pudding goo. Not that it would've been difficult for that to happen anyway but, the point is, I was caught off guard.

"The hell? No way that's going to happen," I protested. "You're a hero. You saved my life."

"Like it or not, I'm three hundred years out of date. I'm obsolete. I am, at best, a museum piece. I'm a machine, I've done what I was built to do, and now I will be decommissioned."

"The hell you will!" I shouted. "Ship, I've just come into a shit-ton of cash. How about we get you some fancy upgrades and maybe a cool robot body?"

Ship took a long time to respond. "You would do that for me?"

"Hey, you saved my life. The least I can do is return the favor," I said. I gestured at the display screens. "Pull up some cyber catalogs or whatever and let's go shopping."

So we did. And then some. Ship got some sweet new upgrades. Nothing too wild, though. I mean, Ship was still Ship, just *more*. I got some upgrades too. To be honest, we both looked pretty damn hot.

Ship and I, we went through a lot together. That sort of thing changes you, makes you see things differently.

And, sure, I'm *mostly* organic and Ship's *mostly* synthetic, but that doesn't seem to be a big deal anymore. And, well, it's been legal on most worlds for at least a century, so…

Notes on "Rock Band"

I really painted myself into a corner with this one. Three sentences in and I had the protagonist stuck in a dead spaceship, alone and probably doomed. How do you get out of that?

I cheated a bit and changed the tense on the second sentence.

I introduced the ship's computer just so there'd be some sort of dialog going on. The computer, like everything on the ship, is a compromise between the corporations who want to maximize their profit margin, and a union who wants to keep its members alive …and paying dues. So, on average, everything is just barely adequate. On average. I guess what I'm saying is, Ship isn't exactly state-of-the-art A.I. and the ship itself is a flying deathtrap.

I'd half-considered making up a union specifically for space transport but then figured the Teamsters have been around for over a century. What's a few more?

I fully expected the protagonist to die alone in space. It wasn't until I started thinking about what the cargo might be that it occurred to me that it might be the key to being rescued.

I did some rough calculations on orbital timing and stuff. Probably got them wrong, but hopefully close enough that my astronomer friends won't yell at me too badly.

By the way, in this universe, almost every world has an Aldrin City. The Space Race went on a bit longer here, and Buzz Aldrin ended up being the first person to set foot on Mars. It was a one-way trip, though, so the crew spent the rest of their lives on Mars, exploring, and setting up habitats for the next wave of colonists. There's statues of Buzz everywhere.

The ending was a bit of a surprise to me. I was going to leave it as "working class nobody gets into trouble, then makes good". Y'know, if they hadn't nearly gotten killed they'd probably have ended up flipping burgers in a diner on Ganymede. (Pause for a moment to consider the physics of flipping a burger patty at 1/7th Earth's gravity.) And having them end up rescued and rich is an OK ending, I suppose.

But, hey, it's been 300 years and attitudes are different. So, why the hell not turn it into a romantic ending? We're all consenting sentients here, right?

Loaner

Jordan had a great body, until he'd rented it out to pay off his student loans and it'd come back damaged.

"Just look at this mess!" Jordan said, "I've gained ten pounds, my left knee is all messed up, and what the fuck is this tattoo on my ass?"

The clerk peered at him over her glasses. "You've been compensated for any damages incurred during the rental period. If you discover any additional issues during the next 10 days, please file form 10-37 with the Claims department. Good afternoon, Mister Callahan." She gestured toward the exit.

Jordan looked at his pay stub. The extra "compensation" would just barely cover the tattoo removal and a couple weeks of physical therapy to get his knee back in shape. The extra weight wasn't considered "damage", he guessed. The rest of the money would go a long way toward getting him out of debt. *Better than nothing, I guess.* He shrugged, slung his backpack over one shoulder, and left.

The protesters were out in full force today, picketing Animus Unlimited. A woman wearing torn jeans and a beat-up sweater, carrying an "OUR BODIES ARE NOT FOR SALE!" sign rushed up to Jordan and shouted "Abomination!" pointing an accusing finger at his face.

Jordan took a step back, held up his hands and said, "Whoa, hey! I'm not possessed. One hundred percent all-natural, here."

The woman eyed him warily as other protesters gathered to see what all the fuss was about, some cautiously reaching into their pockets for what Jordan could only assume were weapons. His accuser held a clear crystal amulet up to his face. It immediately glowed green.

The woman lowered the amulet, stepped back, and called out, "He's clean!" to the gathered crowd.

Addressing Jordan, she said, "Sorry, can't be too careful these days. Penelope. Most folks call me Penny." She stuck out her hand.

He shook it. "Jordan. What's with...?" He gestured at the amulet.

"This?" she said. "Oh, it detects the possessed. Glows red if there's an unwanted spirit. So, you thinking about becoming a Vessel?"

Jordan rubbed the back of his neck and stared at the sidewalk. "Just finished being one. Didn't exactly go as advertised."

"I've seen those ads," said Penny. "All about 'helping the departed put their affairs in order'. I'm guessing you had a slightly different experience."

"I'll say," Jordan said, looking up at her. "As near as I can tell, some dead guy took my body on a joyride for a week. 'Put their affairs in order' my ass! Which, by the way, now has a brand new unicorn tattoo on it."

Penny suppressed a smirk and instead nodded sympathetically. "Look, there's a Pentacles just around the corner. Want to grab a coffee and tell me about it?"

Jordan shrugged. "Sure, why not?" As they headed toward the coffee shop, he added, "You seem a lot less, um, fanatical than when you jumped me in front of Animus. What's the deal?"

"Oh, that." She chuckled. "The whole 'abomination' thing… it helps rally the troops. Also, it makes me look less threatening."

"*Less* threatening?" Jordan said. "I thought you were going to drive a stake through my heart or something."

The barista called out, "Next in line, please" interrupting their conversation. Penny paid for both orders and they sat down.

"I suppose I should properly introduce myself. My name is Doctor Penelope Ferchmorgan, Prof… *formerly* Professor of High-Energy Magics at Clemson University."

"Clemson. Grimoire Belt college, right?" Jordan said between sips.

Ferchmorgan winced at the slur. "That's a bit harsh."

Jordan shrugged. "Sorry. I suppose I should've been a bit more tactful. You bought me a coffee and all. It's just… I'm feeling a little worked-over, y'know?"

Doctor Ferchmorgan nodded. "Fair enough. Want to tell me about it?"

"Not much to say. I went in, they did some magic stuff, I woke up a week later, feeling like I'd been hit by a truck." Jordan shook his head. "For all I know, I *was* hit by a truck."

Doctor Ferchmorgan leaned forward. "So you were awake for at least *some* of the ritual. What can you remember? Any details would be helpful."

Jordan frowned in concentration. "I was lying on a table. There was a bunch of chanting. I didn't recognize the language. I never took Magics in school. They had a big crystal near my head. I think… I think they put a cage with a mouse in it between me and the crystal." He shook his head. "That's all I remember."

Ferchmorgan nodded, sitting back again. "The blood sacrifice. The death of a mouse would be a sufficient conduit, at close quarters."

"They killed the mouse?" Jordan said. "What a shitty thing to do."

"Mages used to sacrifice humans," she said. "This is a bit of a step up. Anyway, human sacrifices were outlawed in most countries by the 18th century, and pretty much frowned upon long before that."

Jordan narrowed his eyes. "You seem to know an awful lot about this stuff. What gives? What aren't you telling me?"

Doctor Ferchmorgan sighed. "You're right. I do know a lot about this. In a way, all of this," she said, waving her hand in the general direction of nothing. "All of this is my fault."

She leaned forward again and lowered her voice. "But I think I can fix it. I need someone on the inside, though, and that's where *you* come in, if you're up for it."

Jordan sighed and ran his hand though his hair. "Lady, I've got to go back to work on Monday. So I've got tonight and tomorrow to get my shit together and… Wait. What do you mean, this is *your* fault?"

She gestured to Jordan's backpack. "You've got a tablet or something in there, right? Look me up. I'll wait." She sat back.

Jordan eyed the woman warily, pulled out his Golem tablet and searched her name. He found a twenty-year-old news article about a team of magicists working on communicating with the spirit realm. The principal investigator was Penelope Ferchmorgan, PhD. The woman in the photo looked young, much younger and much less rumpled than the gray-haired, disheveled one in front of him, but it was definitely the same person.

He put down the tablet. "No offense, but you haven't aged well."

She laughed. "This? Mostly makeup. I have to *work* at it to look this crappy." She nodded in the general direction of Animus Unlimited. "Last thing I need is for *those* yahoos to recognize me. Besides, they're less likely to take me seriously if I look like one of the crazies."

Jordan tilted his head. "Then why hang out there at all? I mean, if it's so risky, why not just stay away?"

"Like I said, I think I've got a way to fix all this," she said. "But I need someone on the inside."

"Recruiting. And, when you say 'all this', you mean… what, exactly?" He mimicked her vague hand gesture.

"You think this is *normal*? The dead are running this country. Eighty percent of the wealth is in the hands of deceased people's estates." She thumped the table with her index finger. "And ever since Affiliated Spectres, they've been buying elections."

Jordan frowned. "Affiliated Spectres?" he asked her.

She shook her head. "Don't you read the news? Affiliated Spectres v. FEC? No? OK, look… Six years ago, the Supreme Court ruled that a deceased person's estate was legally a person and, as such, could contribute to political campaigns as a form of free speech."

"OK, so dead people are messing with politics." Jordan shrugged. "What's all this got to do with you?"

"I – my team and I – we set this off. We were looking for a way for the spirit realm to communicate more effectively with our world. We came up with a simple, short-term possession spell." Ferchmorgan sighed, looking down. "We never really thought about the consequences, how it might be abused. In retrospect, it seems all so naïve."

"Wow. Starting to get the picture here," said Jordan. "You've got some major guilt over helping a bunch of assholes take over the country, and now you want to fix it. Where do I come in?"

"I need a possessed person. A single body with consciousnesses from both realms. I'm hoping you can help me get that."

Jordan shook his head. "Won't work. When I was possessed, I was *out*. No memory at all. And definitely no control over my body. Can't you just, y'know, kidnap someone who's already possessed?"

"We considered that. They're almost impossible to get access to. Major security. These are super-rich dead folks, after all. They can afford the best bodyguards, even when it's not *their* body being guarded."

"OK, yeah, I can see that," Jordan said. "So what makes you think you can get access to me when *I'm* possessed? I'm going to be in the same state as any of those other people." He raised his index finger, as if to interrupt. "And that's *assuming* I'm in, which I haven't decided yet, OK?"

"Ever since the Affiliated Spectres ruling, I've been working on a way to stop them," she said. "I've just *now* come up with the last piece to the puzzle." She leaned across the table and lowered her voice to just barely above a whisper. "I can arrange for someone – you, for example – to regain control of your body while a possession is still in progress. How does that sound?"

A wicked grin played over Jordan's face. "That sounds pretty damn interesting."

Doctor Ferchmorgan grinned back. "So, are you in?"

Jordan stared off into space for a while. It was awfully tempting. He had no idea who'd been using his body for the past week, but he was pretty sure he hated the dead bastard. Payback would be pretty sweet.

"I need to think it over for a while," he said finally. "Anyway, I'll need to get back in shape before they'll let me do another gig. And I'll need to take another week off work."

Ferchmorgan nodded. "Fair enough. You can find me here," she said, handing over a business card. "I work late. Come after hours, any time between six and ten. West entrance. It'll be locked but I can buzz you in. Don't bother calling ahead."

Jordan took the card and stood up. "OK, I'll think about it. Thanks for the coffee."

Ferchmorgan stood and shook his hand. "Any time. I hope to hear from you soon."

Over the next few weeks, Jordan kept his social life to a minimum, falling into a routine of work, physical therapy, diet, and tattoo removal treatments. *Painful* tattoo removal. Every treatment, every pass of the mage's wand, every crackle of the ink removal spell, pushed him to seek revenge. It *had* to be a unicorn, didn't it? Just about any other tattoo would've been tolerable, but a *unicorn*? That had to go. *Ugly, smelly beasts.*

On a Monday evening, after a particularly painful de-unicorning session, Jordan grabbed a bite to eat, then took a cab downtown, having it drop him off a couple blocks from the Museum of Supernatural Sciences. He walked the rest of the way, figuring it best not to tip off too many people about where he was going. Doctor Ferchmorgan seemed to be nervous about letting the wrong people know something was up. She was probably right. She was dealing with powerful people, dead or not.

He found the west entrance: a steel door with an intercom and a small sign that said "Service Entrance. No Soliciting." He pushed the button. A few seconds later, a voice – probably hers – said, "Yes?"

He leaned in to speak. "It's Jordan. From the coffee shop." No reply but the door buzzed open. He stepped inside and found himself at the bottom of a stairwell. Take the stairs or try the interior door? He decided to wait and see if someone would come get him.

Eventually, he heard a door open somewhere above him. "Jordan? Come on up. Third floor."

Fortunately, his knee was pretty much back to normal. The two flights of stairs weren't much of a chore. He needed the exercise anyway. *Two more pounds to go.* Doctor Ferchmorgan was waiting on the third floor landing, holding the door open.

She looked very different. More like the photos of her online. He'd expected a lab coat, though. Instead, she wore neatly pressed khakis and a Clemson Gorgons sweatshirt. She smiled as he approached. "Jordan! Good to see you. You're looking much more rested than the last time we met."

"Yeah, I clean up good," he said. "So do you, Doctor Ferchmorgan." She really did. The makeup and gray hair she'd had on when he first saw her made her look much older than she was. Looking at her now, he'd guess late thirties, maybe forty. That would've made her a teenager when she led that research team. Kid genius or something.

"Oh! That's right. I was in full 'scary old lady' mode, wasn't I?" She laughed. "So, I'm guessing your presence here means you're in? And Penny's fine. *Doctor* Penny, if it makes you feel better."

Jordan nodded. "Yeah, let's do this. Whatever 'this' is. I'm still not clear on that." He looked around the room. Book shelves, cabinets, workbenches strewn with tagged artifacts. Nothing you wouldn't expect in a museum workroom.

Doctor Ferchmorgan – he really couldn't bring himself to think of her as Penny – pulled out a small black case, set it on one of the few clear spots on the workbenches, and opened it. There were seven vials in there, and indentations for three more. She picked up a vial and handed it to Jordan.

He held it up and examined it. It contained a single, fairly large capsule. "Am I supposed to *swallow* that thing?" he asked.

"Yes, sorry," Ferchmorgan said. "That's as small as I could make it and still ensure it'd work. The capsule will allow you to take control while you're possessed."

Jordan began to open the vial but the Doctor Ferchmorgan stopped him. "No! Not yet. After you swallow it, the capsule will take about an hour to dissolve. At that point, the spell will activate. Take it as close to the transfer as you can. We don't want it going off before the possession begins. Ideally, I'd like you outside Animus' facility before you wake up."

"Ah, OK," Jordan said, pocketing the vial. "And when I *do* wake up…?"

"Come straight here," Doctor Ferchmorgan said. "Buzz in, just like you did tonight."

Jordan nodded. Simple enough. "What happens when I get here?"

Penny sat down and motioned for Jordan to do the same. "That's where things get a bit dicey," she said. "Jordan, I'm going to attempt to disconnect this realm from the spirit realm. If it works, the dead won't be able to interfere with the living ever again."

"Holy crap!" Jordan gaped at her. "That's big. That's amazing."

"*If* it works, yes. It could change everything," she said. "When are you going in again?"

"I'm pretty sure I can schedule something for next weekend. I'll call Animus tomorrow and set up an appointment. If they've got a gig for me, I'll put in for time off at work and we should be ready to go."

"Great," Ferchmorgan said. "Look, I really appreciate your going through with this. Any last questions?"

"Yeah. One." Jordan looked at the case of vials. "What happened to the other three?"

"Oh!" she said. "Don't worry. It's not like anyone's met with a horrible fate or anything. I just recruited several people. So far, you're the fourth to show up here." She shrugged. "Nobody's been able to schedule an appointment yet. There's a good chance you'll be the first."

That made him feel a bit better. "Gotcha." He headed toward the exit. "If all goes well, I'll see you back here on Saturday."

Tuesday morning, he called Animus Unlimited. They practically jumped at the chance to schedule him. Apparently his previous 'occupant' had been asking about a repeat possession. Creep. Dead creep. He hung up and scheduled his PTO.

The week passed slowly. Jordan stuck to his routine, though. He didn't think anyone was watching him but there was no point in drawing attention to himself.

Saturday morning, he made his way to Animus. There were a few protesters outside but Doctor Ferchmorgan was nowhere in sight. He headed in.

This time, he was familiar with the process, at least. Sign in, fill out the forms, sign the release. He was then led to a small changing room with a shower stall and an open lockbox. A hospital gown and bath towel hung on clothes hooks.

He knew what to do but the attendant told him anyway, reciting the instructions in a voice that simultaneously conveyed professionalism, boredom and disdain. "Please disrobe completely, including all removable jewelry. Place all your belongings in the lockbox, close it firmly, and key in a four digit PIN. Shower thoroughly and put on the gown. When you're ready, push the call button and wait for an attendant to come get you. Do not leave unless accompanied by an attendant."

Jordan stripped down, carefully palming the capsule before locking away his clothes and backpack. He stepped into the shower and yawned, slipping the capsule into his mouth and using his hand to channel the shower's water after it. He just barely managed to choke it down. He showered quickly, toweled dry, slipped on the gown and hit the call button. An attendant appeared almost immediately.

"All set!" said Jordan brightly. *Let's get this moving. Clock's ticking.*

He was led to the ritual room, really not that much different from a typical doctor's examining room. Animus Unlimited didn't go in for theatrics. The attendant directed him to lie on the padded table, even though he'd already begun to do so. The attendant left and returned with a large crystal that gave off a dim blue glow, placed it on a pedestal next to Jordan's head, then left.

Jordan lay there for what seemed like hours. *Come on, come on. Tick tock.*

Finally, a mage entered, carrying a small cage which she placed between Jordan and the crystal. This time, Jordan noticed that the mouse was not free to roam around the cage. It was restrained, its neck positioned directly below a small blade. The bottom of the cage was lined with plastic, presumably to catch the blood.

The mage held up a clipboard and read the incantation in a monotone, ticking off checkboxes as she completed each stage of the ritual. Finally, she lowered the clipboard and reached for something just below Jordan's line of sight. He heard a small click, followed by a wet thunk. Everything went black…

…and he awoke in the back of a limousine. Jordan flinched at the abrupt change, even though he was expecting it. A large, well-dressed man sat across from him.

"Is everything alright, sir?" the hulking man asked.

Think fast. "Yes. Fine. Just an itch. I don't think this one showered properly. Ha ha." He looked down at what he was wearing: a very nice suit, perfectly tailored, probably worth more than he made in a year.

The man, presumably a bodyguard, nodded. "Understood. Directly to the hotel, then?"

Jordan mused briefly on the connotations of the term "bodyguard" in this particular situation, then said, "No. Slight change of plans. I need to go to the Museum of Supernatural Sciences. I have some… unfinished business there."

The bodyguard nodded again. "Understood." He pressed the intercom button and gave the chauffeur the new destination.

Just before arriving, Jordan remembered to specify the West entrance. The bodyguard relayed the instructions without so much as a raised eyebrow.

The limo pulled up to the entrance and the chauffeur immediately jumped out and held the door for the two passengers. Jordan walked up to the steel door, turned to the huge man and said, "I'll need to do this alone. Wait here and make sure no one else enters." *Nice touch.*

He turned back to the door and pressed the button. A short pause and then, "Yes?"

"It's… it's me," he said. The door buzzed open and he entered.

Once inside, he realized that the feeling of being watched that had been haunting him since he'd woken up didn't go away, even though he was now alone. He had chalked it up to being shadowed by the bodyguard but now realized it was something else entirely. He wasn't *alone* in his body. Someone else was in there, and not terribly pleased about it.

He made his way up to the third floor, where Doctor Ferchmorgan was waiting for him. As he approached, she held up an amulet, the same one she'd used on him outside of Animus' offices. It glowed red.

She held up a hand to stop him. "Wait. How do I know it's you?"

Jordan thought about that for a minute, then said, "chai latte and mocha decaf", their Pentacles order.

Ferchmorgan relaxed a bit. "OK, come on in. We have to work quickly. There's not much time."

"Why? Is the spell going to wear off or something?" Jordan asked her.

"No," she said. "My lab mate Gerald's on lunch break. He'll be back in half an hour. Really don't need *him* stumbling into this." She saw his blank look and added, "Jordan, I work here as a *curator*. This necromancy stuff is all off the books."

"Right," he said. "I guess I didn't really think about that. So, what do I need to do?"

"Stand right there," she said, pointing to a ring of five wooden workbench stools. Jordan complied.

Doctor Ferchmorgan placed a crystal on top of each stool, stepped back and chanted, "gadewch yr hawl un allan". The crystals glowed violet.

"OK Jordan," she said. "Walk slowly toward me. You'll feel a slight tugging."

He stepped out of the ring of stools. *Slight tugging?* It felt like his insides were being ripped out through his spine. The connection suddenly broke and he stumbled forward.

"Ow! What the hell was…" he began, turning to look behind him. Standing in the middle of the ring was a vaguely human-shaped column of mist. And it looked seriously pissed off. It gesticulated wildly but made no sound.

"So far, so good." Ferchmorgan handed him a pair of sunglasses. "Here. You're going to need these for this next bit."

Jordan pointed to the ghostly figure. "So, *that's* who was occupying my body?"

"Yes. And he doesn't seem to be too happy about the current situation." Ferchmorgan fetched a metal tray and placed it on the floor just outside the ring. "OK, here's where things get a bit iffy."

"*Iffy?* You didn't say anything about iffy," Jordan said. "Exactly *how* iffy are we talking?"

Doctor Ferchmorgan placed a large wooden block in the middle of the tray. An eye bolt was screwed into the side, with a length of twine leading from it. She stood up and addressed Jordan.

"There's a lot of uncertainty with what I'm doing here. I'm working under the assumption that the spirit realm is, well, artificial."

"It's fake?" Jordan asked.

"No, not *fake*. Just, um, *constructed*. I don't think it always existed. I don't even think it's *supposed* to exist. There are no references to it prior to the fifth century. I think it was created around that time and, along with it, much of the magics we depend on day to day." She shrugged. "It's not a popular opinion, in the magicist community."

"What I'm attempting to do, using your friend here as a conduit, is to cut off the connection between our realm and the spirit realm." She pulled a large crystal out of a locked cabinet and placed it on one side of the wooden block. It didn't seem to glow at all, but his eyes ached when he looked at it.

"I figure one of four things is going to happen," she continued. "One: This fails completely, your former occupant blabs to Animus, and we both get into a shitload of trouble."

"Not loving option one," said Jordan.

"Same here," said Ferchmorgan. "Two: All connections between the two realms sever and the dead no longer have control over our affairs."

She continued, "Three: The link between realms is severed and the spirit realm ceases to exist. This could potentially cause magics to stop working as well. That could be extremely disruptive to the economy."

"Option two is still my favorite so far," Jordan said. "I'm afraid to ask what option four is."

"That's the most severe, I'm afraid," Doctor Ferchmorgan said, placing a second crystal on the opposite side of the wooden block. Jordan noticed the two crystals were drawn toward each other, clamping the block between them. "It's *possible* what will happen is that the spirit realm will cease to *ever* have existed. I have no idea what would happen in that case. It could potentially change the entire world. Rewrite the past sixteen hundred years of history."

"That..." said Jordan. "That's pretty fucked up. I'm still rooting for option two. I can't imagine a world where magics doesn't exist. I mean, how would we manage to get *anything* done?"

"If that happens, I guess we'll adapt. Will have adapted." Ferchmorgan pulled a large bone from a drawer. She noticed Jordan's puzzled look and said, shrugging, "Dragon femur. I just need something long and non-conductive."

She used the bone to push the tray into the middle of the circle. The specter seemed to shrink away from the assembled components but, trapped in the circle, had very little room to maneuver.

"OK, here goes," she said, discarding the bone and grabbing the end of the twine. "You should put on those sunglasses now." Jordan complied.

Doctor Ferchmorgan braced herself, chanted "dinistrio'r deyrnas ysbryd", and pulled hard on the twine, yanking the wooden block out of the circle.

The two crystals slammed together, emitting a brilliant flash of light.

Jordan was just thinking how glad he was that he had those sunglasses on, when the room started to swirl around him and he found himself…

…standing on a street corner. Nothing looked familiar. He looked at the street signs. Salisbury and Lenoir. He should be right out in front of Animus Unlimited. There was a parking lot instead.

No, wait. There'd *always* been a parking lot there. Hadn't there?

How did he get here anyway? He was just at the museum. He felt the need to get back there.

He pulled his Golem tablet… no, his *Android* tablet from his backpack, and looked up the Museum of Supernatural Sciences. No, not "*Super*natural". There it was on the map: Museum of *Natural* Sciences. Just a fifteen minute walk. He stopped at Pentacles… *Starbucks*… on the way.

As he walked, he felt disoriented. Everything seemed both strange and familiar at the same time. "It could change everything," she'd said. *Who'd* said that? Someone. Someone important.

He noticed a number of other people looked equally confused. But, hey, it was downtown on a Saturday afternoon. That was pretty much the norm.

He passed a shabbily-dressed man, muttering to himself. The man glanced up briefly and said, "They're all dead now," then continued his muttering.

While waiting to cross Davie Street, he overheard a small girl enthusiastically telling her father about the unicorn she saw yesterday, and how it was gone now. Her father, distracted by something on his phone, mumbled, "That's nice, honey."

By the time Jordan got to the museum, he could barely remember why he had to be there. He stood at the west entrance, staring at the steel door for some time, and then pressed the intercom button.

A vaguely familiar voice answered, "Yes?"

Jordan didn't know what to say. He looked down at the cups in his hands. Why did he have *two*? "Um, chai latte and mocha decaf?"

There was a long pause, then, "Right. Um… Right." The door buzzed open and Jordan entered.

"It could change everything." Maybe not *everything*. He started up the stairs.

Notes on "Loaner"

I spent a bit of time trying to decide if the body rental thing was going to be technological or magical. It ended up somewhere in between. I had assumed the clients were old rich people. And that quickly got changed to *dead* rich people.

The idea that the spirit realm was something created relatively recently didn't occur to me until fairly late in the process. I picked the 5th century because, y'know, Merlin and stuff.

The story essentially takes place in two universes: one where the spirit realm (and magic) popped into being during the 5th century, and, well, *this* one. Magic doesn't exist here, but some folks still have vague memories of the alternate universe. Like y'do.

Indistinguishable From Magic

My wealthy (and a bit dotty) aunt had left me, her favorite niece, a battered wooden box containing exactly one twig. Almost everything else had been donated to various charities, and I was the only blood relative who actually got *anything*, so it was difficult to be bitter.

And, to be fair, "twig" was a less-than-gracious description. The sum total of my inheritance was as follows:

- one ancient wooden box that had, by the looks of it, been repaired and re-varnished at least a dozen times

- one tapered wooden stick, roughly nine inches long, with a silver knob on the thick end

- three stone pellets, about half an inch long and a quarter inch in diameter

- one neatly-folded piece of tissue-thin, rose-scented paper, with the words "Use it well" written in precise cursive hand

Use it well. How do you use a stick *well*?

I sighed, boxed up the various bits and pieces, and went to put it in the trunk I'd reserved for the various artifacts Aunt Celia had sent me from her travels. I tucked the box into the jumble of boxes, bags and books already in there. Before closing the lid, though, I fished out the photo album lying on top. I sat down on my bed and flipped through it.

The photos were all either taken of or taken by Aunt Celia. Some were very old, dating back to when she was in her teens. A lot of them had been transferred from one album to another, as they either filled up or wore out. The current one was nearly full. I felt a twinge of sadness, realizing it wasn't going to get any fuller.

I was staring at a page about halfway through the album – not really looking at the pictures, just staring into space – when one of the pictures caught my eye. Aunt Celia was standing in front of a theater, below a marquee for "Fahrenheit 451". She was all dressed up: evening gown, pearls, hair done up.

She always wore her hair up. Always. She could be wearing coveralls and boots, and still her hair would be up, twisted into an elaborate bun… That's when I saw it: the glint of silver in her hair.

I started flipping backwards through the album… 60s… 50s… 40s… She'd started wearing her hair like that in 1946, around the time she turned 20. And in every single photo – at least the ones where the angle was right – there it was: a bright silver knob, sticking out of the top right side of her hairdo. I flipped forward, right to the end. The same silver knob in every picture.

How had I never noticed that before? Granted, I had only known her for the past couple decades of that but you'd think that'd be something you'd notice, right? I mean, sure, I knew she always wore her hair up and there was always something shiny in it. It just never occurred to me that it was the *same* shiny something. She'd worn the same hair stick for seventy years. And now that hair stick was in my trunk.

What did it mean? Clearly it was important to her, and giving it to me must have been significant. But, "use it well"? I barely had long enough hair to make a decent ponytail, let alone an elaborate updo. I put the photo album away and pulled out the box again, laying out its contents on the kitchen table, under better lighting.

I examined the stick more closely, looking for inscriptions, anything that might indicate why Aunt Celia thought it so special. The stick had three indentations, equally-spaced around the shaft, near the fat end. Each indentation was inlaid with a stone oval, the same speckled stone as the pellets. No. Not quite.

I fiddled with the silver knob until it came loose. Note to self: Push in and turn to unlock. I tilted the stick, and out slid a cylindrical pellet, identical to the three in the box. The end was hollow, and the indentations had oval windows opening into the cavity. Curiouser and curiouser. I tried putting the other pellets in place and each fit perfectly. Interchangeable decorations? But they were all the same. Why have four identical decorative inlays? I put the original back in place and locked the silver cap over the stick's end.

I picked up the stick, holding it by the fat end. My thumb, index and middle finger slipped easily into the indentations, touching the cool stone. The sliver knob rested comfortably in my palm.

"Oh, I know! It's a magic wand!" I said, laughing.

I waved it around. "Bippity, boppity…"

BOOM

When the spots in front of my eyes cleared and my ears stopped ringing, I examined the gaping hole in my kitchen wall. "There goes my security deposit."

I carefully, ever so gently, laid the wand back in its box and closed the lid. I sat at the kitchen table for some time, alternately staring at the box and the hole in the wall. At least I didn't hit any pipes or wiring.

I needed help. I pulled out my phone and texted the first person who came to mind.

Got a serious problem. Need your help.

What's up?

Aunt Celia left me her magic wand.

Bullshit.

I took a picture of the hole in my wall and sent it.

Bring it here. And bring wine.

Be right there.

I headed over to Meg's house with the box and three bottles of Cabernet. She met me at the front door.

"Let's see it," she said, practically yanking the box from my hands. I followed her into the kitchen. She has a *much* nicer kitchen than mine. She has a much nicer everything than me. Meg's a freelance tech consultant and makes a killing at it.

She set the box down on the kitchen table and started examining it while I uncorked a bottle and poured us a couple of glasses.

Meg looked up at me, peering over her glasses. "This thing's ancient. You should have it appraised on Antiques Roadshow or something. Why bring it to me?"

"Meg, it blew a hole in my wall. It's definitely dangerous, probably magic." I shrugged. "You're the first person I thought of. The stuff you make, it's the closest thing to magic *I've* ever seen."

It's true. I've seen her make everything from battling robots to a tiny radio-controlled butterfly. And that's just the stuff she does for fun.

Meg laughed. "Clarke's third law."

I stared at her. "Huh?"

"Any sufficiently advanced technology is indistinguishable from magic," she explained. She opened the box. "This doesn't look very high tech, though. I need to take a closer look at this stuff."

She carried the box into her office/lab and set it down on a work table. I followed with the wine glasses. Priorities. "Don't you want to see how it works?" I asked.

"Not yet. For one thing, I saw what it did to your wall. Don't want that happening in there," she said, nodding toward the kitchen. "Re-tiling that would be a serious pain."

She picked up my aunt's note, examining it closely. "Besides, I don't like to play with a new toy until I've read the instructions first."

"It's three words," I said, sipping my wine. "Not exactly heavy reading."

"Yeah, that's what's visible," Meg said, pulling out a heat gun and directing it at the paper.

"What," I laughed, "You think she wrote a secret message in invisible ink?"

Meg nodded. "I've met Aunt Celia. Clever old bird. One of the smartest people I've ever met."

"Really? I always thought she was a bit loopy."

"The two aren't mutually exclusive." She put the heat gun away and retrieved a black light. "There we go!"

Written around the edge of the paper, in neat, glowing cursive, were the words, "Look in the bottom of the box."

"Well, shit," I said. "I never would've thought of that."

"That's why they pay me the big bucks." Meg carefully removed the remaining contents of the box and started poking around inside. "Oh, here we go. False bottom."

"Oh come on," I scoffed. "This is starting to feel like one of those National Treasure movies. What's next, a map leading to the Hidden Pyramids of Antarctica?"

"See for yourself," Meg said, pulling out two documents. One was old and brown, covered in runic script, and sealed in plastic. The other just looked like a sheet of regular printer paper. Meg unfolded the latter. "I'm guessing *this* is a translation of *that*."

"OK, yeah, just shows how to hold it – you already figured that out the hard way – and then goes on to say you can manipulate objects by carefully applying pressure to the indentations. Oh! And there's a sort of force-feedback element to it. You can detect objects at a distance through your fingertips."

"Huh, cool. I hadn't noticed that," I said. We'd both finished our wine, so I headed back into the kitchen for the bottle.

"That's because you were too busy blowing up your apartment," Meg called from the other room.

"Yeah, laugh it up," I said. "I'd like to see you do better."

"So would I," she mumbled. She put everything back in the box and headed down the hall. "Let's go to the workshop," she called back to me. "Bring the bottle. Actually, bring all three. This might take a while."

"Wait, I thought *that* was your workshop," I said, indicating the room we'd just been in.

"You think I build those big honkin' sumo-bots in there?" Meg said, opening a door and flicking on a light switch. "Nope. *This* is where all the magic happens."

We headed down a staircase into a huge room. And I mean huge. It was easily as big as the house itself. It looked like a techie's wonderland. Dozens of workbenches, a milling machine, laser cutter, at least two 3D printers, on and on.

Near the center was a wet bar, complete with bar stools and a mini fridge. I unloaded my armload of wine bottles on it, and poured us a couple more glasses.

Meg set the box down on a relatively clean workbench, and pulled out the wand. "OK, let's see what this baby can do." She carried it over to...

"Meg," I said warily, "Why do you have a cinder-block wall in your lab?"

The thing was about six feet wide, stacked two deep, and stretched most of the way to the ceiling. It was covered in scorch marks and pitted with precise round holes of various diameters.

Meg grinned at me. "Not all the things I build are safe, you know. Or strictly legal, for that matter. That's why..."

"...they pay you the big bucks," I finished.

She stood facing the wall, about ten feet back. I took up a position behind and to the left of her, well out of the line of fire.

Meg aimed at the center of the wall and squeezed. A blue glowing circle flashed briefly on the surface of the wall, making a low *whump* sound.

"Interesting," she said. "Let's give it a bit more juice." She took aim again.

I picked myself up off the floor and, when my eyesight and hearing had sufficiently recovered, I said, "Right, I should've mentioned that. There's a bit of flash and boom with that thing."

"I'll say!" Meg was examining the damage to the wall. It didn't have an actual hole in it, but several blocks had been pushed back, causing the center to bow inward. The blocks closest to the center were badly damaged but more or less intact.

She turned her attention to the wand. "What I want to know is, where did all that energy come from?"

"Magic!" I laughed. Hey, I'd already had a couple glasses of wine and been knocked to the floor twice today. I was in a pretty silly mood.

Meg wasn't. "Yeah, magic…" she muttered. She retrieved a small meter and waved it over the damaged wall. "Not radioactive, at least."

"You have a Geiger counter?" I asked.

"Of course. Like I said, not everything I build is safe," she explained. She held up the meter. "It also detects neutron flux but that would've…"

Meg took the meter and the wand over to the wet bar, poured a glass of water, set it down, and put the meter beside it. She aimed the wand at the glass and gently squeezed it. The water bubbled as if carbonated and glowed blue briefly.

"Huh," Meg said. "No gamma radiation but a whole bunch of neutrons."

"Care to translate that into regular-person language?" I asked.

"I don't know," she said. "It's like there's a nuclear reaction – could be fission or fusion – but no ionizing radiation. Let me try something…" She went and grabbed another meter.

"Another fancy detector gadget?" I asked. Trying to keep up with Meg's thought processes was like watching a swarm of bees. There was definitely a purpose to it but there was also a lot of chaotic buzzing.

"Thermometer," she said, sticking the probe in the water. "23 degrees." She caught my reaction. "*Celsius,*" she added.

She pointed the wand at the glass again and applied pressure to the indentations. "Trying just a little bit of constant pressure this time."

The water fizzed again and glowed steadily.

"30 degrees… 40… 50… 60… 70… 80… 90…"

The water started to steam, then boil. Meg put down the wand, turned to me and started grinning. "No gamma, lots of neutrons and a hell of a temperature increase. You know what this means?"

"Does it involve thirty-five foot long Twinkies?" I asked.

Meg laughed. "No. Well, kinda, in the sense of there being a hell of a lot of energy bottled up in this. I just boiled a glass of water using no external energy source and minimal effort on my part." She waved the wand at me (yeah, I ducked). "You get enough of these things, you could run a steam turbine."

"Well, we've got one," I pointed out. "Oh, and three spare stones."

"Right," she said. "Let's look at those…" She went back over to the workbench, picked up one of the stones and gave it the three-fingered pinch.

She dropped it immediately. "Ow! Fuck! Ow!" She ran to the bar and stuck her hand under the faucet.

"You OK?" I asked.

"Yeah, just a little scorched," she said. "Well, three things learned from that. One: Never do that. Two: The stones are the key component. Three: The rest of the wand isn't just decoration. Let's have a look inside." She picked up the wand and twisted the knob.

"Push down and turn counterclockwise," I said helpfully.

"Got it." She examined the silver end-piece. "Huh. The inside of this thing is a polished parabolic mirror. I bet *that's* not a coincidence. I mean, who'd polish the *inside* of an end-cap if it wasn't necessary? OK, so, process of elimination…"

Meg tried the pinch maneuver again, this time holding the silver knob behind it. One of the wine bottles slid a few inches. She was getting good at controlling it, I noted with only a tiny bit of envy.

"Nice!" she said. "So, stone slug plus parabolic reflector equals magic wand. The wood's just there to hold it all together." She reassembled the wand, this time with the other stone in it. It appeared to work the same as before. "So, why four slugs and only one wand?"

"Maybe there used to be more wands," I suggested.

Meg nodded. "We could easily build three more out of stuff I've got around here…" She stared off into space for a moment. "Or maybe something a bit more interesting."

She grabbed a notepad and started to sketch something that looked like a satellite dish with a six-pointed star in the center. "We take one of the slugs, put it in a girdle of linear actuators and back it with a reflector. I'm guessing polished aluminum will do."

I kinda understood where she was going with this. "So, the linear actuators play stand-in for fingertips. Can they detect force-feedback?"

"What? Oh! We haven't even tried that, have we?" She handed me the wand. "Here. I've been hogging it, haven't I? Give it a try."

I held the wand, being careful not to squeeze, and waved it around. "So, what am I supposed to... Oh!" I could feel something in my fingertips. I closed my eyes and concentrated. "It's weird. It's like I'm running my fingers over whatever the wand is pointed at. It's kinda... um... blurry, but I can make out some shapes."

"Yeah, the instructions say that it takes years of practice to perfect the technique," Meg said. "But maybe, if I wrapped a piezoelectric sensor array around the slug, I could make some sort of imaging rig."

I rubbed my eyes. "That sounds all very techie and fascinating but I'm beat, and I've had three... four glasses of wine. Can I crash here? Not really in any shape to drive."

"Sure," she said, barely looking up from her notepad. "You know where the guestroom is. Make yourself at home. I'm... I'm going to stay up a bit longer."

I smiled. "I figured you might." She was in the zone. I'd just be getting underfoot.

I woke up the next morning, rumpled and a bit disoriented. I cleaned myself up a bit, made coffee, and went in search of Meg. She was still in the workshop, hunched over a bench, soldering something.

"Did you sleep *at all*?" I asked, handing her a cup.

She looked up, startled at the interruption. "What? Oh, thanks," she said, taking the coffee from me. "Yeah, I napped for a bit at one point. Got caught up in this thing." She waved her hand at the room in general.

The place was transformed. All of the half-finished projects on the various workbenches had disappeared, replaced by four satellite-dish-shaped devices like her original sketch. There were dozens of additional sketches on sheets of paper scattered about. For someone who built a lot of high-tech devices, Meg still seemed to prefer paper-and-pencil for design work. Everybody has their quirks, I guess.

"You've been busy," I said, making the understatement of the year. "Care to tell me what these things do?"

Despite having almost no sleep, Meg was full of manic energy. She bounded back and forth among the four devices. "Each of these are essentially the same sort of setup, but optimized for different purposes. And each one is a thousand times more powerful than the wand is."

She gestured to one. "This one can, given a sample of a material, scan its surroundings and locate more of the same. Basically, anything that's *not* what it's looking for is transparent, making it really easy to find what you're looking for. That could be used for anything from medical scanning to locating mineral deposits."

Over to the next. "This one can cut through anything, at any distance. The current rig is accurate to within a millimeter but I could easily upgrade that to sub-micron, with the right parts. Handy for precision manufacturing or, coupled with the other one, mining the resources you've located. Hell, you might even be able to do surgery on someone without opening them up."

"These," she said, gesturing to the last two, "are capable of levitating and moving large objects."

"You've got to be kidding," I said.

"Watch…" she said, and typed a few commands on a keyboard. One of the dishes spun around to point at the cinder-block wall. It slowly lifted, rotated upside down, and settled back on the floor. In the process, the blocks were rearranged so that they no longer bowed in.

"Holy shit!" I said. "That was awesome! Wait… why do you have *two* of those? And what about that free energy thing? Did you make a prototype of that?"

Meg looked askance. "Yeah, I can make one of those fairly easily, but right now, we need these four and we've only got four slugs."

I could tell something was up. "OK, what's going on? Is this a good news/bad news thing?"

She shrugged. "Yeah, that's probably the best way to tell it. The good news is, I was able to calibrate the scanner to find the exact material used in the slugs themselves. That will allow us to make more slugs to be used in all sorts of devices. I've got enough ideas for about fifty basic patents. I'm putting you down as co-inventor on all these, by the way. Only fair. Also, since we're currently the only ones who know the 'secret ingredient', we can corner the market."

I grinned. "So, we can make a whole bunch of devices, sell them, plus sell the slugs to anyone who wants to make their own stuff. And, we collect royalties from them anyway. We'll be rich!"

Meg nodded. "Yeah. Filthy rich."

She didn't look all that happy. "So, what's the bad news?"

She walked over to a PC, one of many scattered around the workshop, and pulled up Maps. "The bad news is, the exact type of stone we need is rare, really rare. I scanned the entire planet and was able to find only one source."

"You scanned the *entire* world?" I asked. "How powerful *is* that thing?"

"Pretty damned powerful," she said. "I spent a lot of time last night getting that kind of range out of it."

"So, the bad news is the one source is buried deep beneath the ground somewhere or something?"

"No," Meg sighed. "That would've been reasonably easy to work with. This is much worse. The one source of this stuff is here." She pointed to the screen.

"What, *all* of it?" I asked.

"No, just this one here," she said, pointing to the screen. "It's the only one that's an exact match. Go figure. The wand slugs were probably made from broken-off pieces."

"Oh, just one," I said. "That's not so bad then." I looked her in the eyes. "We *can't.*"

"We *have* to."

"Someone will notice. What am I saying? *Everyone* will notice!"

"We can replace it with an exact replica, made from similar stone. I've already had one carved out." Meg patted the Number Two device, the cutting machine.

That's when it dawned on me. "The two levitation machines. You need them to make the swap. We'll never get away with it. We'll get caught."

Meg waved her hands at the room in general. "How? We'll be operating the whole thing from here, thousands of miles away. Even if someone *does* see a couple of rocks move, there'd be no way to tie it back to us. Oh, sure, the original will be here so we can carve it up, but I've already dug a pit in the back yard. It'll be buried before anyone knows it's gone."

Still being negative, I asked, "And how exactly do you plan to *get* it here?"

She brought up a map. "I'm going to fly it in, low enough to avoid air traffic, high enough to avoid ships. Over land, it'll take rural roads, just below the tree line. And boom, it plops down here. Good thing I've got a big lot and lots of trees."

I leaned against the bar and put my face in my hands. "You've got this all figured out, haven't you?"

"Hey, that's why they…" she began.

"Yeah, I know." I sat and considered my options for a while. I turned back to Meg.

"How many slugs can we make from that?" I asked.

"With no waste, about six million. Probably closer to five." She smiled, knowing I was coming around on this.

"We'd have the market cornered. Exclusive rights," I said.

"Yes."

"We'd be rich."

"Filthy rich."

"I could quit my job."

"Yes," Meg said. "Well, you'd have a new one: CEO of Bluestone Energetics LLC."

"Not in love with the company name, but…"

"Yes?" Meg said, leaning forward.

"Fuck it. Let's give it a shot," I said. "It'll be the biggest heist in history. How could we *not* do it? When do we start?"

"Tonight," she said. "Everything's set up and ready to go."

"Jeez, you really *were* busy last night!" I said. "So, what do we need to do?"

"Pretty much just sit back and watch the show," Meg said. "I've got the whole thing pre-programmed."

"And what time does the show start?"

"About five," Meg said. "I figure we'll be done by about three A.M."

"OK, I'll head home, get cleaned up, and change," I said, heading toward the stairs. I paused. "We're going to need more wine."

"And pizza," Meg added. "I'll order that if you'll pick up the wine."

Now, before you go judging me, keep this in mind: We changed the world. Sure, we got enormously rich off this, but look at all the good we did. Cheap, clean energy. Medicine was transformed overnight; almost no one dies of disease anymore. The ability to manipulate weather patterns eliminated drought.

And, yes, *flying cars*. Goddamn flying cars. The first few million slugs went into important stuff but, once Meg learned how to synthesize them, they started showing up in consumer products.

We nearly got caught. There were hundreds of UFO reports that night. The tabloids reported a several witnesses seeing flying rocks, but most were drunk or stoned at the time. Saturday night, after all.

Yes, what we did was technically wrong, and definitely illegal. But, in the end, the world is much better off than it was. And that's what's important, right?

And the visitors to Stonehenge? I doubt any of them can tell which one of those rocks is fake.

Notes on "Indistinguishable From Magic"

I'd written a very similar story a few years ago, with the same title. Was never quite happy with how it turned out. I like this one better.

Wasn't sure how much to give away in this one. I was going to mention "bluestone" or "spotted dolerite" but figured that'd give away the ending.

And, yeah, I did calculate the number of stone cylinders you could get from one of the bluestones at Stonehenge. Hope I did the calculations right.

Meg might seem like an unrealistic character: incredibly talented, resourceful and mischievous. I know at least three people almost exactly like Meg. If in the unlikely event I inherit a magic wand, I'll contact one of them first. And, yeah, I'll bring the wine.

The Butler Did It

"So that guy, whose brain was used as the template for nearly every robot servant in the world, was a serial killer," Mark said, between bites of his club sandwich. "They only found out after he died and his relatives were going through his stuff. Newspaper clippings, photographs, pickled body parts…"

"Um… Trying to eat, here," Tanya interjected, picking at her mahi mahi salad. "Maybe ease up a bit on the whole 'body parts' thing?"

"Right. Sorry." said Mark.

Janine chimed in with, "But it's weird, right? Sutcliffe interviewed thousands of candidates. All sorts of tests and shit. And they ended up picking a complete psycho." She snapped her fingers at a passing waiter. "Hey! Running a bit low on Pinot Noir."

"Right away, ma'am," the robot said, hurrying away to fetch another bottle. Our third so far.

"You could be a little more polite, you know," I pointed out.

Janine waved her hand dismissively. "It's just a *robot*. It's not like you can hurt its feelings. Just a pile of nuts and bolts."

"…modeled after a psycho killer." Mark being morbid again.

"So, what, our waiter's going to murder me because I didn't say please and thank you?" Janine snorted. Pretty sure Janine had been drinking the majority of the wine.

"Sutcliffe just put out a press release saying there's no danger. Their robots are inhibited from causing any harm," Tanya said, flipping though the news stream on her tablet.

"Well, they *would* say that, wouldn't they?" Mark said. "What else *could* they do, slap a label on each model that says 'Warning: May cause unexpected disembowelment'?"

"Still eating, Mark," said Tanya.

"Sorry. But, look, they *have* to spin this. They can't have people thinking their products are unsafe. I mean, they're *everywhere*. The entire staff of this restaurant are Sutcliffes." Mark waved his arm at the dining area in general, nearly connecting with a waiter, who deftly side-stepped the collision. Mark might've had a few glasses of Pinot, too.

The waiter returned with the wine.

I looked up and said, "Thank you."

"You're quite welcome, sir," the waiter replied, then hurried off to tend to another table.

"You don't *have* to say thank you to those things, Sean," Janine said, directing her gaze unsteadily in my general direction. "It's just a... *thing*."

"I know," I said. "I'm just not comfortable being impolite to something that looks human. I guess I'm worried that I'll get into the habit, and start treating humans like that too."

Mark laughed a bit too loudly, causing some of the other diners to side-eye our table. "You are *so* Canadian."

"No. I get what Sean's saying," said Tanya. "The less human you treat *robots*, the easier it is to start treating *humans* as something... less than human. Look at Janine. She already treats everybody like they're at her beck and call."

"That's got nothing to do with robots," said Mark. "Janine's just an asshole."

"Mark..." I began.

"No, it's true," interrupted Janine. "I *am* an asshole. Always have been. But I get away with it because I'm smart and talented. Oh, and *seriously* hot."

"Can't argue with that," said Tanya, still picking at her salad. I swear, she takes *forever* to eat.

Mark nodded in agreement. "She's got you there, Sean."

I shrugged. "But the point still stands," I said. "It's like, treating robots inhumanely makes *me* feel less human. Or something. I don't know."

"Well, you've certainly swayed me," Janine scoffed. "Say, were you on the debate team in college? Because, wow."

"Oh, look. Tanya's finally finished eating her salad," Mark interjected. "*Now* can we talk about the gory Mister Randolph?"

"Hold on," said Tanya, pouring a glass of wine. She downed it quickly and braced herself. "OK, *go.*"

Charles Leonard Randolph was the human template for all of Sutcliffe Robotics' domestic robots. Up until ten years ago, Sutcliffe had specialized in industrial robots. They had avoided getting into the domestic robot arena, which was probably a good move on their part. There were dozens of manufacturers, hundreds of models, and they all had one thing in common: they were nearly useless.

The A.I. processors in these early domestic robots were plenty powerful. More than enough for handling most household tasks. They just didn't have any common sense. The general approach to programming was to start with an out-of-the box A.I. template, usually something about the equivalent of a five-year-old in intelligence and world experience. Then they'd take that, bolt it into a humanoid frame and try to teach it to be a butler or maid or waiter, from scratch.

This approach worked fairly well, up to a point. They could handle most routine domestic tasks, the key word here being "routine". Slight deviations in their routine would throw them off-task, and their behavior would continue to diverge from the norm until a human intervened and set them back on course.

For example, a broken dustpan might cause a robot to sweep a pile of dirt around in circles for hours, while the roast in the oven burned. Or construction on a sidewalk might divert the robot's path to the point where it was wandering around the HOV lane on the interstate. That actually happened. Seriously. The news footage of the resulting traffic jam was really something to see.

The Butler Did It

In short, domestic robots were stuck firmly in the "trough of disillusionment" on the technology hype curve. They seemed really cool but, in the long run, were more trouble than they were worth.

While all this was going on, Sutcliffe Robotics was quietly acquiring a startup called Cerebragraph which claimed to be able to record memories into permanent storage. Their goal was to eventually provide brain backups with the hope of eventually restoring to a new body. Technological immortality, of a sort. Sutcliffe had other plans.

Again, very quietly, and using a third-party agency, Sutcliffe started interviewing domestic workers. The agency was purportedly searching for "the perfect butler" to be the subject of a documentary about the latest of a long line of vocations being replaced by technology. The winning candidate was a seventy-year-old man named Charles Randolph, who had been in the service of the Bonneville family – essentially his entire life – taking over his father's position when he retired. Even though the Bonnevilles' fortune had dwindled over the years, Charles had stayed on out of loyalty, and at reduced wages, up until his retirement. He was exactly the sort of person Sutcliffe was looking for.

Sutcliffe offered Mr. Randolph a huge sum of money for two things. One: a scan of his brain, and two: his complete discretion. Randolph happily agreed to the terms and, true to his word, kept his mouth shut. The man was good at keeping secrets, after all. He'd had a lifetime of experience.

It was only after his death that everyone found out who Charles Leonard Randolph was, and exactly how good he was at keeping secrets. Over the years, Randolph had killed over forty people. His relatives found a diary, cataloging every murder in meticulous and often explicit detail. He had also kept a souvenir body part of each victim, preserved in mason jars. A finger from one, an ear from another, an eye, a nose, a tongue. There was a distinct five-senses theme.

All of this hit the newsfeeds last night. Social media streams were clogged with news, information, misinformation, speculation, opinion, and (of course) extremely tasteless memes. Sutcliffe Robotics was frantically working on damage control. My friends and I were still trying to process all of this when we met for our regular Sunday brunch.

Mark eagerly went over all the gory details, both verified and rumored. Tanya cringed, expressed disgust, and made a respectable attempt at catching up with Mark and Janine on wine consumption. Janine interjected rude comments and laughed inappropriately.

Me? I'm the "quiet one" of the group. I was also way behind everyone else on the wine. I tried to be the voice of reason, but wasn't sure reason really applied in a situation like this. We were having brunch while *literally surrounded* by robots modeled on a serial killer. Does that sound reasonable?

I really didn't know how to feel. The Sutcliffe Jeeves line was the most popular domestic robot in the world. From the day they were introduced, they completely dominated the market. Everyone had one. Janine, for example, had just traded up to the Jeeves S7. Mark and Tanya both had S6's. I was still on the old S4 but had been saving up for an S5. Like I said, everyone had one.

I'd been staring off into space for a while, when something Tanya said pulled me out of it.

"It's just so surreal," she said. "I mean, imagine waking up one day and finding out your toaster was made from old landmine parts. You'd always be thinking, this time, instead of making a nice piece of toast, maybe it'll blow your face off."

"I don't even know if I *have* a toaster," Janine said. "My S7 takes care of all that stuff."

Tanya grabbed her by the arm and glared at her. "That's. Exactly. My. Point." She punctuated each word with a shake of Janine's arm, causing her head to wobble slightly.

I looked around the restaurant. "We've been here a long time," I said. "Maybe we should get the check. Free up the table?"

The other three looked down, played with their forks or wine glasses. Did everything except look me in the eye.

Right. I always was a bit slow on the uptake. Getting the check meant leaving. Leaving meant going home. Going home meant being alone …nearly alone …alone with a robot.

"Or we could stick around and order another bottle?" I offered.

Notes on "The Butler Did It"

This one was fun. I got to play with robots, serial killers, and drunken brunch conversation.

I knew from line one, what this was going to be about: The dawning horror of finding out that something familiar, something you rely on every day, is suddenly potentially lethal. In my newsfeed, I have a product recall section. It's amazing how many of them contain the phrase "due to laceration hazard".

I wasn't sure how to end this, but then it dawned on me that each of these people, very probably young single professionals, lived alone. And the last place you'd want to be on a day like this is *home*. Alone. With a robot. "Warning: May cause unexpected disembowelment."

I'd love to see a YouTube video made from this. It'd be easy. It's basically four people having brunch. You'd need lots of extras and a couple people dressed as robot waiters. I'm pretty sure Tanya should be played by Shirley Henderson. Think we could get her?

Imaginary

Newborns see the universe as it really is, completely unfiltered. That's why they scream so much. By age 3, our brains have learned to pick out the "real world" from the noise and chatter of the countless parallel "imaginary" worlds swirling around us. Bobby never quite managed to do that.

It was pretty clear, early on, that Bobby was different. His parents noticed he was often distracted by things that weren't there. See, Bobby had a lot of imaginary friends. Most of them were also named Bobby, and looked just like him. His parents thought this was very cute, showed a remarkable imagination and, yes, seemed just a little weird.

The thing was, Bobby's friends *were* imaginary, just not in the usual sense. These friends – these other Bobbys – were imaginary in the same way that the square root of -1 is imaginary. They existed at right angles to reality.

There were at least a hundred Bobbys, maybe more. They sort of faded out the farther away they got. No, "farther away" wasn't quite right. They were here but... not. Bobby didn't have words for it.

One time, when he was six, Miss Gwen from down the street was babysitting Bobby while Mommy and Daddy went out. Miss Gwen liked to hear stories about the other Bobbys.

"Do they talk to you?" she asked. She was in a chair reading a big thick book. Bobby was playing on the floor with the other Bobbys.

"Yes." He could see and hear a few other Bobbys answer the same question. He couldn't see the other Miss Gwens, though. Maybe Miss Gwen didn't have any imaginary friends.

She asked him another question. "Do they ever tell you to do bad things?"

"What sort of bad things?" Bobby asked, puzzled by the silliness of the question. Why would a Bobby tell another Bobby to do something bad?

"Do they ever tell you to hurt people?" Miss Gwen seemed very worried about something. She kept fiddling with her necklace, the one with the man sleeping on the letter "t".

Bobby laughed. "Oh no. All the Bobbys are nice, like me."

Miss Gwen relaxed a bit. "Do... do the Bobbys have halos? Or... wings?"

He laughed again. "They don't have wings! They're *boys*, not *birds*! ... What's a halo?"

Miss Gwen smiled. Bobby thought Miss Gwen was pretty. "A halo is a beautiful glow around your head."

One of the Bobbys said "like a space helmet" and the rest of them laughed.

"No," said Bobby. "None of their heads glow. They're just like me."

"Are they here now?"

"Yes."

"Where are they?"

"Right *here*."

Miss Gwen frowned. "I can't see them, Bobby. Can you point to one of them for me?"

Bobby raised his pointer finger, and twisted his hand this way and that. He started to cry. Other Bobbys cried too.

Miss Gwen picked him up and put him on her lap. She held him in her arms and stroked his hair. "What's wrong, Bobby? Why are you crying?"

Bobby sniffed. "My finger won't point in that direction."

Miss Gwen didn't say anything. She held him for a while until he calmed down. Bobby climbed down off her lap and started playing again. Miss Gwen picked up her book again.

One of the Bobbys said something that made Bobby laugh and say, "No, Daddy wouldn't do that."

Miss Gwen looked over the top of her book.

Imaginary

Bobby looked up at her and said, "Bobby just told me he saw you and Daddy kissing yesterday. I told him that was silly."

Miss Gwen slowly put down her book. "I think play time is over. Time for bed."

Bobby thought it was a bit early for bed, but a lot of the other Bobbys were going too, so it must be OK.

Miss Gwen didn't come to babysit anymore after that.

As Bobby got older, he learned to keep his mouth shut about the other Bobbys. Mom and Dad thought he was too old to have imaginary friends. The kids at school thought it was weird. Bobby pretended the others weren't there most of the time. He learned to tune them out and concentrate on the *real* world. When one of them wanted to talk, though, they'd all find a quiet place where no one else could hear and hold a Bobby Meeting.

This worked really well for a long time, until The Accident. Bobby was ten and Dad had taken him downtown to the Science Museum. It was great. Other Bobbys were there too, but they all ignored each other.

Afterward, Bobby and Dad were waiting to cross the street. The signal changed to "walk" and Bobby stepped off the curb. Dad grabbed him and yanked him back, just as a truck barreled through the intersection.

Some Bobbys' Dads were too slow. Some Bobbys didn't get pulled back in time.

Twenty-three. Twenty-three Bobbys went flying, crumpled up by the trucks in their worlds. Bobby couldn't see the other trucks, just the bodies. Bobby screamed. He sat down on the sidewalk, looking at the scattered Bobbys, and cried and screamed and cried. He stared at the bodies, watching each fade out as its Bobby-ness left it. Dad had to carry him back to the car.

Bobby had to start going to a therapist. It didn't really help. What could he say? "Oh, I just saw a couple dozen of me get hit by a truck." They'd lock him up. So he kept his mouth shut.

But, every year on that day, Accident Day, they held a Bobby Meeting to remember the ones who died.

When Bob was in high school – he was "Bob" now; "Bobby" was a kid's name – he learned about imaginary numbers. He called a Bob Meeting. The name of that changed too.

"So, are we all imaginary? Like imaginary numbers?" several asked.

"I think so," said one Bob. "We all go off in one direction, but it's not a direction you can point to. It's not *real*."

"We're *complex*," some said. Others laughed at the pun.

One Bob said, "Wait… we all go off in *one* direction. Can any of you see any Bobs on the *other* side of me?" There weren't really *sides* but there wasn't a word for it, so "side" had to do. All the Bobs shook their heads or said "no".

"That means I'm the first one," the same Bob said. "I'm Bob Prime."

Some Bobs agreed. Some rolled their eyes. A couple called him Bob Zero. Others laughed at that.

Bob could tell, Bob Prime was going to be insufferable after that.

Bob, all the Bobs, started reading up on imaginary numbers, then complex numbers, then extra dimensions, Many-Worlds theories. They began to realize that each of them was real, each of them lived in a separate timeline, and, for some reason, they were aware of each other.

Bob tried to get into the Advanced Sciences track but his grades weren't good enough. Calculus made his head hurt. Instead, he studied on his own, finding what he could in bookstores and the library. He tried contacting some scientists about it but they never returned his letters. Well, Richard Feynman sent him an autographed picture, but that really wasn't much help.

None of the Bobs were smart enough to make sense of the complex physics involved. Most went into engineering or computer science. Bob Prime dropped out of college, joined a punk band, and changed his name to Bob Zero. Bob found it hard to tune him out when he was performing. After one particularly loud night of music, booze and drugs, Bob Zero passed out and never woke up. Bob felt sad about that but – and he wasn't proud of this – a little relieved.

Most of the Bobs got office jobs. Some got married. Some got divorced. Some played the lottery. None of them ever won.

Bob eventually got internet access. It was still new and there wasn't a lot on there, but there *were* some discussion boards. He found other people who said they could see into other dimensions. Most of them were lying, or delusional, Bob thought. There was nobody else on Earth – *this* Earth – quite like Bob.

Bob spent a lot of time reading sci-fi books and watching movies about time travel. He read a book called "Crossing the Streams" that *almost* got it right. He wondered if the author had similar experiences or just a really good imagination. He tried contacting the author but he had died years ago.

Bob would occasionally reflect on how he essentially had a superpower, but had completely failed to make any use of it. He just didn't have the imagination or ambition to do anything with it. He'd wasted his one gift. And he'd wasted his life …all their lives.

The Bobs had health problems. High cholesterol, high blood pressure. Some took medicines; some didn't. Some collapsed at their desks. Some went to sleep and never woke up. Over the years, one by one, the Bobs died off.

Eventually, there were only two left. They sat on a park bench and talked. Nobody really took notice. Just another old man sitting on a park bench, holding a bundle of flowers, talking to himself.

"Not much of a Bob Meeting."

"Nope. Just the two of us now."

"One of us is going to be the last, you know."

"Yeah."

They sat there in silence for a while.

"I guess we should go. It's time."

They got up from the bench and walked. Out of the park and down toward the Science Museum. It was Accident Day.

On the way, one of them started coughing. He had to stop and catch his breath.

"You OK?"

"I'm fine. It's nothing." He stood there, hands on knees, wheezing.

They stopped on the street corner by the museum. The corner where the first twenty three of them had died, years ago. So many years ago.

The two knelt down in unison and placed their flowers on the corner. Pedestrians walked around them, pretending not to notice the shabby old man.

Bob got up slowly. His joints ached.

The other Bob didn't get up. He slowly fell onto his side and lay there, curled up and wheezing.

"Bob?" Bob said.

The other Bob didn't answer. He didn't move. He even stopped wheezing. Stopped breathing. Bob stared at the body, watching it fade out.

He stood there crying for some time. A little girl asked her father, "Why's that man crying?" Her father, staring pointedly at his phone, didn't answer her.

Bob started to walk home.

"It's a long walk," he said to no one. There was no one to talk to. He kept talking anyway.

"I'm all alone now. I've never been alone before. I wonder what that's like. So far, it seems pretty awful."

A young man with a backpack nearly ran into him. Bob looked up briefly and said, "They're all dead now." The man looked surprised, started to say something, then hurried on his way.

"He's probably in a rush to be somewhere. Got places to go. Probably has someone waiting for him."

Bob had no one. For the first time ever, Bob had no one.

Notes on "Imaginary"

Yeah, this one turned out to be a bit of a downer. It started off as a silly story about someone who was in constant contact with his parallel selves, a continuum of Bobs. But it quickly devolved into a story of attrition.

I'd kinda like to see Bill Mumy, at all his various ages, play Bob. All you'd need is a video camera, a really well planned out shot list, and a time machine. Somebody get on that, OK?

Oh, and yeah, the little girl and guy with the backpack make an appearance in another story.

Monster

No one ever really expects to find an actual monster in their kid's closet, especially not a werewolf in a tracksuit.

"I can explain," he said. He held up his hands (possibly paws) in surrender.

"I seriously doubt that," I replied. "You're a werewolf and you're hiding in my daughter's closet."

"Ah, well, where I come from, this spot is located in my lab."

"OK. One: That doesn't make any sense at all. And, two: you'd better come up with a better explanation than that before I call the police. Or Animal Control."

"This is going to take a bit of time. Perhaps if I came out of here and you put down the club?" he suggested.

I looked at the baseball bat in my hand. "OK, come on out. But I'm keeping the bat."

The werewolf stepped out into Lisa's bedroom. In the better lighting, he looked a bit less wolfish. Definitely not human, though. I'd seen a lot of amazing cosplay and makeup effects but *this*? This looked real.

"Are you a monster?" asked Lisa, peeking over her comforter.

The werewolf turned to face her. "No, I'm a scientist."

"Oh, OK. I like scientists. Goodnight," she said, turned over and went back to sleep. Kids. Go figure.

I gestured toward the bedroom door, still keeping my bat handy. He exited the room, still keeping his hands visible. Closing the door behind me, I directed him down the hall to the kitchen. I mean where else are you going to interrogate a werewolf intruder at 5am?

"So, you were saying that your lab is in my kid's closet…" I said. Sitting at my kitchen table, he seemed a lot less threatening, and quite a bit more nerdy.

"Sort of," the wolf replied. "The closet and the lab share the same spacial coordinates, but in different timestreams."

I closed my eyes and shook my head slowly. "I can tell I'm going to need a coffee to hear the rest of this. Want one?"

"Yes please," he said.

I started the coffee maker and pulled two cups out of the cupboard. "Are all the people in your 'timestream' werewolves, or are you just *special?*"

"Everyone is like me, yes," he said. "That's the primary reason I'm here, if you get my meaning."

"No, I really, really don't," I said. "You're going to need to fill in a few blank spots for me. Let's start with why you decided to show up in a kid's closet in the middle of the night."

"It's mid-afternoon where I'm from," he explained. "There must be some temporal slippage between the streams. It's March third here, yes?"

"May fifth."

"May fifth, 2107?"

"2016."

"Oh dear. Nearly a hundred years' difference," said Mr. Wolf. "When I saw the doll, I had assumed you were more advanced and had found a way to reverse the effects of Maladeloup. We've investigated several parallel timelines and this is the first one that showed any promise at all."

I facepalmed at that. "OK, back that up again and start over. What's Maladcloup and what's a doll got to do with it?"

"Right, of course," he said. "Maladeloup is a genetic disease that afflicts the entire population of Earth ...*my* Earth. The first cases were recorded in France in 1823, hence the name. Prior to that, all humans looked like you."

"What, so this disease just suddenly turned everyone into Teen Wolf?" It was really difficult for me to feel sympathetic, given the circumstances. I had to go downstairs and open the shop in a couple hours and I obviously wasn't getting any more sleep tonight.

I put the cups of coffee on the table and sat down across from him.

Wolfy shook his head. "No, not overnight. But it did spread quickly. The last natural human died sometime around 1935."

Oh shit. "You're not contagious, are you?" My skin started to itch. I could feel my hair starting to grow.

"Oh! No, no," he assured me. "We found a cure for the virus years ago. You're in no danger."

"If you found a cure, why do you still look like that?" I waved my cup at him.

The wolf shrugged. "It's in our gene line now. I personally never contracted the virus, but I inherited its genetic alterations from my parents."

I sat back and regarded my "guest" for a moment. "A virus that turns everyone into werewolves and, even if you cure it, your kids inherit it. That seems awfully specific."

He nodded. "Biology isn't my specialty but my understanding is that the virus is very sophisticated. Yes. It appears to have been engineered specifically to make superficial physiological changes without causing any real damage to the host."

"You had genetic engineering in the nineteenth century?"

"No. That's the big mystery," the wolfman said. "We've only recently been able to decipher all the mechanisms it used to accomplish this sort of change. Several labs have samples of the virus, studying it to see if we can re-engineer it to reverse the changes."

"But no luck, huh?" I asked, finishing off my coffee.

"One of the problems is, we'd need samples of unaltered human DNA, and we haven't had access to that in nearly two centuries."

I looked at him and raised an eyebrow.

I saw realization dawn on his face, even through all the fur. "You have an entire planet full of unaltered human DNA samples."

"Yep," I replied. "How many do you need?"

"I'd have to check with our biologists but probably a hundred or so," he said. "Could you get that many volunteers?"

I grinned. "I have an idea how I could, yeah. Can you get back here a week from Saturday? That's…" I mentally counted. "…nine days from now. About two hours later than you showed up this time. We'll need time to set up."

"I think I can manage that. If it means getting DNA samples, I'm sure my superiors will spare no expense," he said.

"Great!" I said. "Do you have a way of collecting DNA samples non-intrusively? Our techniques are a bit gross. Blood or saliva samples." I made a face.

He nodded. "I can get a sampler that requires only skin contact. Totally painless."

I stood up. "Good. Now, if you wouldn't mind, I need a picture of you. Stand over there, against that wall… Turn your head just a bit… Perfect."

After I took a couple pictures, he said, "I need to get back. Same way I came in, I'm afraid."

"OK, we'll just need to be quiet," I said. "By the way, I didn't catch your name. Mine's Rebecca."

"Lorne." We shook hands. His was very furry. Strange sensation. "I can't thank you enough for this. And I'm terribly sorry about frightening your daughter." He paused. "I have to say, you're taking all of this extremely well."

I shrugged. "You meet all kinds in my line of business."

"Which is?"

"Oh! I run a costume shop. It's just downstairs," I said, pointing toward the floor.

I walked him back to my daughter's closet. "One last thing," I whispered, taking care not to wake Lisa. "That tracksuit won't cut it. You're, what, a 40 Regular?"

He looked confused but nodded.

"Perfect," I whispered. "See you next week."

He pulled out a small, oval device and pressed a button on it. He disappeared. No whoosh, no flash of light, just gone.

I spent the next week promoting the event. I 'shopped up a poster with Lorne's picture on it. "Meet a Real Live Werewolf!" I had some high school students paper the local streets. I saturated social media with promotional messages, targeting cosplayers, LARPers, tabletop gamers, sci-fi groups.

On the day, at seven AM, I was in my daughter's bedroom, waiting. Right on schedule, Lorne showed up. But he had a guest.

"I wasn't expecting two of you," I said. They were both dressed in jeans and sweatshirts. The other werewolf appeared to be a woman.

"Yes, sorry," Lorne said. "I really hated to spring this on you at the last moment, but Miriam insisted on coming."

"Well. Hello Miriam," I said, shaking her hand. "To what do I owe this unexpected pleasure?"

"I apologize for the intrusion." She pulled a silver wedge-shaped device from her satchel. "The DNA sampler is an expensive and complex instrument. I needed to ensure it's used properly."

Lorne nodded at Miriam. "Our genetics expert. She didn't feel comfortable entrusting their precious equipment to a lowly temporal physicist."

"Damn straight," said Miriam. Turning towards me, she asked, "So, where should we set up?"

"Downstairs," I said, leading them out of the room.

"Is your daughter not around today?" Lorne asked.

"She's with her father this weekend," I replied. "She'll be disappointed she didn't get to talk to you. She's a big fan of science."

"Yes, she mentioned. And baseball, apparently," added Lorne, nodding to the bat, still propped up in the kitchen.

We made our way down to the shop. I'd set up a "meet and greet" table in one corner of the shop. "Oh! We'll need two chairs, won't we?" I went to fetch one.

When I returned, Miriam asked, "So, we're supposed to just sit here and take DNA samples? I'm not sure how all this is supposed to work."

"Just be yourselves. Talk to the customers, have your picture taken with them," I said. "This is a costume shop. Everyone will assume it's really good prosthetic makeup. And, if anyone asks who you are and what you're doing, just tell the truth. Oh, and try not to open your mouths too wide. Dead giveaway." No point in scaring the customers.

"But first," I said, beckoning them to the back of the shop, "we need to get you some more interesting outfits."

We tried a bunch of different looks. Everything from Medieval to futuristic. Space suits got rejected right off the bat. They were hot and made them look like Star Wars cantina extras. We finally settled on Victorian.

"Steampunk werewolves," I said, adding brass accessories. "I like it!"

Lorne and Miriam took their places, and I got down to the business of opening up the shop.

They were a huge hit. Everyone thought they were "in character" and played along. When Miriam requested a DNA sample, most complied, happy to be part of the "act".

Lots of folks had their picture taken with the pair. I'd set up a nice forest backdrop in anticipation of that. I charged $5 a pop. What the hell, might as well make a few bucks out of the deal.

One of my regulars, Ellie, stopped me to rave about them. "They're amazing! It must've taken *forever* to do their makeup."

"Oh, you would not believe!" I said, grinning.

The place was packed for most of the day. I had to fend off the crowds every so often, so that the "performers" could take a break.

During one such break, Miriam approached me and said, "Someone actually asked me for my autograph. I have no idea what they think they can do with that." I just laughed. Some of my customers can get a bit overenthusiastic.

At one point, I was ringing up a customer when I overheard someone speaking very loudly and argumentatively with Lorne.

"Look, the whole backstory, it just doesn't work. An engineered virus created a hundred years before you even knew what DNA was? Who engineered it, aliens?"

Lorne replied, "We have no idea. Extraterrestrials are, unfortunately, the most likely explanation."

"Oh, sure, it's aliens. Any time you get stuck with a plot hole, trot out the aliens. E.T. ex machina!"

I made my way over to rescue Lorne. Todd was leaning on the table, getting right in Lorne's face. Of course it was Todd. Todd was our resident expert in Everything That's Wrong With Science Fiction. He also often very rude. I noticed Miriam was pointedly ignoring them and still taking samples.

As I approached, I politely but firmly said, "Todd, Lorne? Could I see you both in the back room for a moment please?"

Both men looked up, startled (and looking a bit guilty). They followed me into the back.

"Todd," I said, "we've discussed this before. If you want to continue coming into *my shop*, you need to behave in a polite and respectful manner at all times." Nicest guy in the world when he was happy but, when he was nit-picking about sci-fi, he could be a serious asshole.

I turned to the wolfman. "Lorne, show Todd the inside of your mouth. Stick out your tongue and say 'ah', please."

Lorne complied. Todd turned white.

"So, the lesson here," I continued, "is that even reality has plot holes sometimes."

Lorne closed his mouth again. Todd kept staring. "Does… does anyone else know?" he asked.

"No, and we'd like to keep it that way," I said. "Lorne and Miriam are taking a considerable risk being here, so we'd like to keep it quiet."

Todd grinned. "By hiding them in plain sight. I love it!" And suddenly Todd was happy again. Turning to Lorne, he said, "Sorry about the third degree. And, don't worry, I'll keep your secret. But… um…"

"Yes?" said Lorne.

"Could I get a picture with you and Miriam?" he asked sheepishly.

The rest of the day went relatively smoothly. Todd stuck around to watch the action. He was much more amiable now that he was in on the secret. At slow points, he'd query the pair on details of their world.

After closing the shop, the two scientists changed back into their street clothes, and I escorted them back to the closet.

"I can't thank you enough for your help," Miriam said. "The samples we collected today should give us enough information to reverse the effects of Maladeloup."

"I'm glad I could be of help," I said. "Let me know how things go, OK?"

Lorne shook his head. "I'm afraid this is goodbye. We were only allowed funding for this project because of what was at stake. It's unlikely we'll be able to visit again."

"Oh," I said. "Well… um… good luck, then."

"We did want to give you something in return for all your help," Miriam said, pulling a couple of tablets out of her satchel.

I was going to point out that today was my best sales day in years but thought better of it and accepted the gifts graciously. "What are they?"

"Interactive tablets," said Miriam. "This one is pre-loaded with a series of science courses, from elementary school level, through college. We thought your daughter might appreciate it."

"She'll love it. Thank you," I said. "And this one?"

Lorne shrugged. "We weren't sure what to get you, so this one is loaded with music."

"Well, thank you. That's very nice," I said, trying to imagine what werewolf music might sound like.

We finished our goodbyes and they disappeared.

Over the next few days, Lisa and I played with our respective gifts. Lisa loved the science lessons and was already whizzing through them, well above her grade level. The music, well, some of the pop songs were a bit odd but there were lots of really good classical works. I could probably sell the rights to a few of them.

I also noticed that the tablets never seemed to need recharging, but assumed they had some sort of advanced power source. They were about a hundred years ahead of us, technology wise. A hundred years ahead…

I put down my tablet and looked over at Lisa. "Sweetie, may I borrow your tablet for a moment?"

She shrugged. "Sure." She handed it over.

Most of the early lessons were pretty standard stuff. I scrolled through the table of contents and picked out some of the more advanced stuff. There were lessons in here about stuff I'd never even heard of. I even did web searches. Their world was way ahead of us in nearly every field.

I sat there staring at the tablet for some time. The tablet itself was nearly a century more advanced than anything on this Earth. Probably hundreds of patents. Its contents, though…

Eventually Lisa came over and asked for her tablet back. She saw the look on my face. "Are you OK?" she asked.

I hugged her. "I'm fine, sweetie," I said. "It's just that, if we play our cards right, we're going to be rich."

"Oh," she said, flipping back to the lesson she'd been on. "That'd be nice."

Notes on "Monster"

I'd gotten a few paragraphs into this one, writing under the assumption that the intruder was from an alternate timeline where people evolved from wolves. Then I realized there was no way they'd just happen to speak English. Major plot hole.

So I swapped that plot hole for a less gaping one. OK, the extraterrestrial virus isn't much better, and I'd already used it in another story, But, hey, those Jester ships get around. Anything could happen.

I briefly considered putting something in this one about Lisa asking where all the unicorns had gone to, but it really didn't fit. See, she and her dad had gone to the science museum that Saturday, and she'd seen an old man standing on the street corner, crying over a bundle of flowers.

Death Takes a Lunch Break

Doug caught Death in his bedroom, hunched over, going through his dresser drawers. So he hit it with his tennis racket.

"Ow! That really hurt!" Doug hadn't expected Death's voice to be so whiny. It reached up and rubbed its skull with the bones of its hand, though the two didn't seem to make contact. It turned around to regard him. "Hey, you can see me, can't you?"

"Well, yes. You're standing right in front of me. How did you get in here?" He was still brandishing his tennis racket when a realization crept over him, pushing aside thoughts of defending his home from an intruder. "Am I… am I *dead*?"

"What?" Surprise showed in the voice, if not on the face.

Doug lowered the racket. "Well, you're Death, aren't you?" he said. "Don't people only see Death when they die?"

Death cocked its skull to one side. "Hold on. Let's back it up a bit. What, exactly, do you see when you look at me?"

"You look like Death. A skeleton in a black robe. You know: Death."

Death flapped its arms in frustration. "Oh, lovely! The cloak's on the fritz again. Hold on." Death reached inside the folds of the robe and disappeared, accompanied by an almost inaudible, high-pitched chirp.

Doug swung the racket at where Death had stood, and connected with something solid. By the sound of the grunt, he'd hit Death in the stomach, knocking the wind out of him. It occurred to Doug that Death shouldn't have a stomach …or wind, for that matter. He reached toward the sound of the wheezing, grabbed what felt like a burlap sack and pulled.

Whatever it was gave slightly then was tugged from his grip but not before Doug caught sight of the disembodied head of a young man. He reached out, took a firmer grip and pulled hard. This time, two objects flickered into existence: a black robe in his hand and a man standing in front of him.

The man was in his late twenties, a bit doughy and balding. He wore blue coveralls with a yellow hourglass logo on the sleeve. He was also bent over and wheezing. He staggered over and sat on the edge of the bed. "OK, OK, stop already!" he gasped. He reached into a pocket on his coveralls, pulled out a small foil packet, peeled it open and slapped the contents on his neck. His breathing steadied and he stood up.

The man surveyed the situation. He poked at various nubs on his toolbelt, pulled out a small handheld device, fiddled with it for a moment and sighed.

"What a mess." He looked up at Doug, who'd been standing there, staring and speechless. "I hope you're happy. You know how much paperwork I'll need to fill out when I get back? I'll be lucky if I don't get fired. Ha! A lot *you* care. We're out there, bustin' our asses to save mankind and do you think anyone ever thanks us? No! You don't even know we exist. Nobody in your time period does."

Doug finally found his voice. "What? What do you mean, 'your time period'? Who are you? *What* are you?"

The man seemed to deflate a bit. "I guess it doesn't matter if I tell you. It's not like you're going to tell anyone." He chuckled humorlessly. He wiped his hands on the sides of his coveralls and held out his right hand. "Stan Capshaw, Psyche Retrieval Technician, at your service."

Doug took his hand and shook. "Doug Farrington."

"Oh, you don't have to tell me. I know all about you. Major pain in the ass, you are. Talk about paperwork. Here, buy me a drink and I'll tell you all about it." He gestured toward the kitchen.

Doug had no idea what Stan was talking about but he figured, if he had any chance of finding out what was really going on, it would be by talking to this guy. "Sure. Beer OK?"

Stan grinned. "That'll do nicely."

As they walked into the kitchen, the doorbell rang. The pizza. He'd ordered it just before he heard the noise in the bedroom.

He excused himself and answered the door. As he paid for the pizza, he only vaguely noted that the delivery person was a very attractive woman. Under normal circumstances, he probably would've made an attempt to flirt with her. He would've failed miserably, of course, but at least he would've tried. But these weren't exactly normal circumstances.

He put the pizza on the kitchen table. "You hungry? I was just about to have dinner."

Stan looked at his watch. "Eh, close enough to lunchtime for me. Sure."

Doug took stock of the situation. An hour ago, he'd gotten home from work, ordered dinner and had started to settle in for what was looking like another boring evening. Now, he was sharing pizza and beer with a "Psyche Retrieval Technician", whatever that was. That was as good a place to start as any.

"Alright, so, what is it exactly that you do for a living?"

Stan took a bite of his pizza, washed it down with a swig of beer. "Just like I said. I retrieve psyches. I visit people just before they die and scan their brains. Everything they ever thought or experienced gets stored on one of these." He held up what looked like a marble.

Doug tried to take this in. "So, you collect souls. Like Death."

Stan snorted. "Ha! Yeah, I guess. Never really looked at it that way. It's just a job, y'know? I nip in, scan, nip out. At the end of my shift, I dump the recordings back at the depot and go home. Not like I go around swingin' a scythe or anything."

"But, but, when I walked in on you, you looked like Death," Doug pressed on, "What was that all about?"

"Oh, that? Equipment malfunction. The cloak's supposed to make me invisible. Saves a lot of explaining. 'Hey, what are you doing with that dead guy?' That sort of thing. Sometimes they don't work so well. Like that one." He cocked a thumb in the general direction of the bedroom. "Left my skeleton visible and didn't cloak itself either. Heard about that sort of thing happening. Never happened to me before, though."

"You go around, scanning the brains of the dying and every so often one of your invisibility cloaks malfunctions so that you look exactly like Death? That's a bit of a coincidence, don't you think?"

"Yeah, now that you mention it, it does seem a bit fishy." He stared off into space for a moment, then brightened. "Hey, I've got it! Maybe we're the source of the myth. Maybe people saw the malfunctions and made up the Grim Reaper thing to *explain* it."

Doug looked skeptical. "No, see, that'd only work if you'd been doing this sort of thing for hundreds of years. The legends go way back."

By now Stan was on his fifth slice and third bottle. "Yeah, that sounds about right. I mean, we've only gone back as far as the 1600s but we're extending the range all the time." He saw Doug's puzzled expression. "What, didn't I tell you? We're from the future. Yeah, see, we travel back and forth through time, scanning the dying for the Human Archive Project, Phase One."

"What, you scan *everyone*? Everyone who's ever lived?" He tried to wrap his head around the idea and failed. Too much information all at once. The beer wasn't helping things either.

"Well, no, obviously we can't scan *everyone*. There's been, what, a hundred billion people or so. Takes me about twenty minutes to do one. That'd take, oh, um, well, a lot of overtime, I can tell you." Stan sat back and belched. "No, see, we just take random samples. Pick a few people from here, a few from there. See, we figure future generations will come up with more efficient ways of scanning folks. Probably come up with better cloaking too. Like I said, we're just Phase One."

Stan was on a roll now. "Now, you, Mr. Douglas Albert Farrington. You are a major headache for us. You came up in our random selection… thing a few months back. So, first thing we do is figure out the exact time of death and schedule a pickup. Well, you see, we can't work out your time of death. You don't seem to have one."

Doug jumped. "What? You mean I never die? I'm immortal?" he asked.

Stan laughed. "Nah, nothing like that. You just sort of… disappear. No body, nothing."

Doug's face went pale. It's one thing to find out you're going to die. Everyone does, eventually. But disappearing as well somehow sounded worse. It meant likely not dying of old age.

"So, so, how do I disappear, then? I mean, what are the circumstances?" he said, not entirely certain he wanted to hear the answer.

Stan waggled his fourth beer at Doug. "That's what I'm telling you! We have no idea. See, we can track anybody. Anybody. Plane crash? No problem. We finish the job just before it hits the ground. Lost at sea? In a top secret detention facility? Doesn't matter. We'll find them. But you? You just… vanish. The paperwork we've had to fill out on you! You have no idea. And we can't just sweep it under the rug. You're in the system. We have to process you."

"OK, listen, this is my life you're talking about, so if I sound a bit unsympathetic about your filing problems, cut me some slack, yeah? OK. Now, the important thing for me, see, the *number one* thing for me is, when do I disappear? How much time do I have left?" This was turning out to be a real bitch of an evening.

Stan held up his hands in placation. "Yeah, OK" he said, "you've got a point. I'm not really good at dealing with people one-on-one. Most of the people I meet can't see me. OK, here's the thing. I wasn't sent here today to collect. I was sent to snoop around, find out what was going on in your life. Try to find something we missed. You wouldn't've even known I was here if the cloak hadn't crapped out on me."

Stan leaned forward and tried his best to be sympathetic. "Doug, I don't know how to tell you this except straight out. That pizza girl is the last person to see you. The police report shows that the pizza box was still on the table with one slice left."

Doug jumped up. "What? So that's it? I disappear *tonight*? Sometime between now and tomorrow morning I just go poof? You must know something. Come on, you're from the future."

Stan shrugged. "This is what I'm trying to tell you. We have no idea what happens. We tried everything. We sent monitoring devices back a few times but they kept getting messed up by some temporal anomaly… thing. This is our last shot. I was supposed to come here and dig up some clues. If that didn't work, I was supposed to hide in the corner and watch. I'd write up what I saw, file it and mark the case closed. All nice and neat. Then this…" he gestured at the room "… happened."

"Yeah, OK, so maybe you're part of it now. Maybe something you do causes me to disappear," Doug said.

Stan thought about this. "Yeah, could be."

"Any idea what that would be?" Doug asked.

"Not a clue. Sorry."

Doug sat back down, defeated. "So now what? We just wait?"

Stan shrugged again. "Yeah, I suppose. Listen, I'm sorry about all this. You seem like a decent guy. I mean, y'know, other than the tennis racket thing. I want you to know, if there were anything I could do to help, I would. I just don't know what's going on. I'm as in the dark as you are."

Doug nodded. "Thanks. I appreciate that."

He glanced over at the pizza. Two slices left. Maybe, if no one ate the other piece…

He was still staring at the pizza when he noticed a third person sitting at the table. An attractive, bored-looking woman in her mid-thirties, wearing blue iridescent jumpsuit with a gold hourglass logo on the sleeve. On the table in front of her was a briefcase. She appeared out of nowhere. One second, the chair was empty; the next it wasn't. No flash of light, no whooshing sound, no double-exposure fade-in, the chair didn't even creak. Stan and Doug both looked up with a start.

She introduced herself. "Karen Anders, Anomaly Resolution. I'm with Phase Three. Looks like I've got a bit of cleaning up to do," she said as she unlatched the briefcase. She flipped through papers. "Let's see. Missing death date, equipment malfunction, drinking during work hours, assorted minor paradoxes…"

"Right, then, Mr. Farrington, you'll be coming with me. I'll take you back to my time and we'll get this whole thing sorted out. Mr. Capshaw, gather your equipment and report back to your supervisor." She rattled this off in a monotone, barely glancing up.

Stan found his voice first. "Wait a minute! You can't just walk in here and take over!"

She held up a sheaf of papers. "I can and I have the paperwork to prove it." She pushed back from the table. "Now, if we can…"

Doug had been staring at this woman, trying to remember where he'd seen her before, when it finally dawned on him that he was in the process of being kidnapped. "Hold on. What makes you think I'm just going to…"

The woman reached out, slapped a small disk on Doug's chest and tapped the center of it. He vanished in mid-sentence.

She took a few of the papers from the stack she was holding, paper-clipped them together and put them back in the briefcase. "That's that settled." She looked up. "Now, as for you…"

"Hold on," Stan said, "I've just worked it out. All this mess. His disappearance, the temporal thing. The whole reason I'm here in the first place! You just caused it all by taking him. You're supposed to resolve anomalies, not *cause* them."

Karen shrugged. "Sometimes it's the same thing," she said. "That's time travel for you. Don't worry about it. It'll all work out in the end. Now, *your* job is to make sure you don't leave behind any evidence of your presence here today. Check everything, top to bottom." She glanced at something on her wrist that was probably not just a watch. "I'd better be going. I've got a pizza to deliver. Oh, you'll be needing this." She handed him the remaining pages she was holding. She disappeared before he could ask her about either the papers or the pizza.

Stan flipped through the papers and his face broke into a wide grin. All his paperwork for the day – incident reports, equipment requisitions, everything – all filled out in his own handwriting, already marked "approved" and "expedite". All he had to do was hand it in. Nice. First good news of the day.

He gathered up his equipment, cleaned up half the table so that it looked like Doug had been alone, then did a quick once-over to make sure he didn't miss anything.

Satisfied that all was in order, he started his time belt warming up. Maybe not that whizzy Phase Three tech but it gets the job done. Just as the belt was reaching full charge, he grabbed the next-to-last slice of pizza.

Notes on "Death Takes a Lunch Break"

This is the story I'd already written. The tweet I posted was close enough to the first line of this story that I just went ahead and used it instead.

The title is a play on "Death Takes a Holiday", a 1934 movie that's been remade at least twice, including "Meet Joe Black". This story has absolutely nothing to do with that movie.

The universe in which this story takes place is pretty thoroughly fleshed-out in my head. In the far-flung future, both brain-uploading and time travel have been perfected. A project was initiated to collect the consciousness of each human who has ever lived, as close to the point of their death as possible. Everyone gets uploaded into a vast simulated reality to exist in whatever way they see fit. A technological afterlife.

Residents of the simulation can, if they choose and have the right resources, download into synthetic bodies in order to exit the simulation and interact with the real world. The bodies don't need to be identical to the person's original body. Most people choose a more aesthetically pleasing one.

Karen Anders, being from Phase 3, is a consciousness in a synthetic body. She spends most of her time uploaded but downloads when her work requires it.

Stan Capshaw is from Phase 1. He's a biological human, hasn't been uploaded yet, and doesn't really like his job all that much.

Doug's just some poor schlub stuck in a crappy paradox.

CPSIA information can be obtained
at www.ICGtesting.com
Printed in the USA
LVOW11s1631030117

519590LV00002B/141/P